Miss Moore's Christmas Scandal

Anastasia Hayward

Published by Anastasia Hayward, 2022.

MISS MOORE'S CHRISTMAS SCANDAL

First edition. July 13, 2022.

Written by Anastasia Hayward.

Miss Moore's Christmas Scandal

E ver since she created a scandal at a Christmas ball, Charlotte Moore has dreaded the return of the holiday. For her,
it was another reminder that she didn't quite fit into the con-
fining mold of a proper young lady. This year, at a small Christmas party, Charlotte is tasked with proving to her family that
she can behave within society's expectations or be permanently
exiled to her aunt's rural manor.

Charlotte is determined to stifle her unladylike urges and
act the perfect debutante. But then the very cause of her past
scandal comes knocking at the door and it has in tow the daring, dashing, devil-may-care Henry Simmons.

The rules say to stay away. They say it's not proper to play
games at midnight or get caught alone under the mistletoe.
They also say Charlotte laughs too loudly, dances the wrong
dance, and should not play with fire.

The more time she spends with the handsome rogue, the
more she wonders whether staying on society's nice list is worth
losing the joy in life. Can Charlotte find happiness within the
rules or will following her heart be her biggest scandal yet?

Prologue

The scent of cinnamon swirled with the fresh aroma of evergreen and the dancers mingled in the bright glow of the Christmastide candles. Except for Lord Sudbury, everyone else blurred in her peripherals, blending with the greens and golds and pops of red.

Charlotte tugged on her white silk dress. Mama always dressed her in a boring shade of white, but this time, Charlotte had resewn the hem of the bodice so the dress would be more daring, more her style. So far, her mother had not noticed.

Lord Sudbury handed her another glass, a crystal clear vision of gentlemanly perfection. His clothes were cut of the finest fabric, his hair dashingly curled over his forehead and she so wanted to reach up and brush it over.

Charlotte giggled and sipped her champagne. He had green eyes, the color of Christmas. The color of her wishes coming true.

He smiled at her and her heart beat harder and warmer in her chest, her wish growing.

Would he? Was he going to do what she thought?

The next dance was a waltz, the dance that had flourished in ballrooms, but only for the ladies bold or old enough to dance it.

As a newly introduced debutante, she should not dance the waltz with anyone. She was not allowed.

For the waltz, he would hold her close, his hand on her back for the entire length of the dance while their feet and legs twirled together in time.

She glanced down at his gloved hand on her elbow. He was easily the most desirable man in the room and he was here. With her.

His voice rumbled, stirring something inside her she didn't understand. "I must dance the waltz with the most beautiful maiden here. I haven't been able to take my eyes off you all night."

Mama had warned her that he was too young. To not bother with him because he wasn't out for marriage. Yet here he was, clearly interested in her. Maybe he wasn't too young. Maybe his heart genuinely fluttered just as hers did. Maybe he would whisk her away and they would live an extravagant life together, far from Mama's boring rules.

His dark lashes swept over his cheeks when he blinked and she was caught in his eyes. He stroked her arm and begged, "Please dance with me."

For a moment, her eyes glazed over and she decided she would dance to the end of the world in the pouring rain if that's where he led her.

He smiled a slow, sultry smile that was strong enough to stop her breath. A dangerous smile that promised *fun*.

She set down her drink.

He took her hand.

The beginnings of the triple time counted in her head. *I will waltz, with the lord, of Sud-bury, he will sweep, me off my, slip-pered feet...*

Unlike the men her mama wanted her to dance with, under his jacket, Lord Sudbury was taut and youthful. Romantic. Here in his arms, she could feel how scandalously close they were.

His eyes never left hers so hers never left his. Her skirts twirled around her feet, his lordship never missing a step as his warm hand around her waist guided her through the waltz.

Around her, everything faded to a dull mum, the conversations, murmurs, and clinks of cups fading until the silence of the room enveloped them in a fog.

Was this what it felt like to fall in love? How could she ever dance again with anyone else?

He had said she was the prettiest girl in the room. He had been watching her all night. Her!

Little Miss Moore, from the middle-of-nowhere. Out of all the beautiful ladies, he chose her. She knew she was pretty, she had known she could attract attention, but Lord Sudbury was a different breed. He was, he was...

The strings faded and they stopped in the middle of the dance floor, his arms still around her, his eyes still on hers, and his smile smirking down at her.

That smirk jabbed at her, poked at something and forced her mind to chew on it. It didn't feel right.

Why was he smirking?

She glanced around the room to see everyone staring at her. She, of all of them, had been the one to dance with his lordship.

He led her off the dance floor, the silence of the room beginning to swell in her ears, the ringing in her head making it difficult to put thoughts together.

Now the smirk reached his eyes, his lip curling in a way that drained his charm. What was going on?

Mama grabbed her arm and hissed, "How dare you?"

Mama never let go, tugging Charlotte behind her, through the staring attendees, some of them pointing and glaring from behind their fans.

In the hall, Papa was already waiting and Mama called for their coats. Then she turned and hissed again, "What were you thinking? A waltz? Here and now? Without permission?"

She had known her decision to dance was wrong and she had done it anyway. Lord Sudbury was so handsome, so grand, she had thought everyone would forgive her actions. She hadn't expected him to turn on her.

Like she was a joke.

Her mother wasn't done. "We are disgraced. Your father and I are outside of embarrassed and you cannot begin to comprehend how ashamed you should be."

Oh, she was beginning to comprehend. That fluttering in her chest that had felt so warm and sparkling now faded to a gray lump. She pressed her lips together and reminded herself to keep breathing.

No, that was shuddering. Oh, really, was she going to cry?

Everyone thought she was a fool. Little Miss Moore was willing to dance scandalous waltzes with any handsome lord who glanced her way. She had felt their scornful eyes spearing her and they wouldn't want her around them.

She hugged her cloak around her, the shame creeping down her body like a sticky tar that would never wash off.

In the carriage, Mama said, "I will write your great-aunt and send you to her. You will spend at least the next year with her, but I expect that everyone will still be discussing this next year as well. Your five minutes of flirtation with a rake have cost you your home and family, Charlotte. This is the last straw and it is time you learned to obey the rules of the world you live in."

In the dark of the frigid carriage, Charlotte was glad her parents couldn't see her. She resolved to never again trust a handsome devil. She had just been a joke to him but she would never, ever, let herself be fooled again.

Chapter 1

Christmas was coming. Like a storm from the Atlantic blowing in, with its high unavoidable waves and winds of destructive chaos, the effects of the season would wreak havoc on the lives of those in its wake.

Christmas was coming and, just like a force of nature, Charlotte was helpless to stop it. All she could do was pinch her lips together, clench her fingers, tense her shoulders, and bite out, "Yes, Aunt Johanna. No, Aunt Johanna. Of course, Aunt Johanna. I'm sure he'll have the Christmas goose in time, Aunt Johanna."

Goose. Charlotte scrunched her brows at her paper, smashing the crease down a little harder than necessary. Of all the animals to eat for Christmastide, everyone wanted a goose. And they wanted decorations. Not just any decorations, no, her aunt needed bouquets of folded gold flowers.

"Ow!"

Charlotte glared at the paper cut on her thumb. No one else in the room even looked over.

The widowed Mrs. Katherine Burke scooted closer on the cream-colored sofa to Charlotte's cousin Wallace.

Mrs. Burke, first tugging a lock of dark hair loose so it fell in front of her ear, framing her face, tried again to draw poor cousin Wallace into her conversation, "I suppose you've heard enough about my thoughts on winter fashion. Although I do still think the fichu to be so unnecessary on a lady such as myself," she dragged her fingers across the top of her bosom, "I suppose you would prefer to talk of something more gentlemanly."

She finished her change in topic by pressing her fingers against her lips in a knowing way and looking up at him from beneath her lashes.

Charlotte had known the beautiful Mrs. Burke for less than twenty-four hours and already she was sick of her. The widow had traveled with her late husband's mother. The younger brother who had inherited the Burke fortune had not accompanied them and Aunt Johanna was already lamenting that the party was down one male guest.

Most of the guests hadn't arrived yet and Charlotte was already sick of guests, sick of Christmas, sick of folding gold paper.

All of it.

She looked back up just in time to catch Mrs. Burke resting her hand on Wallace's thigh. Oh, the audacity. For all that he was the ultimate dullard, he didn't deserve what was happening to him. And he probably wouldn't do anything to save himself.

Charlotte cleared her throat. "Mrs. Burke, I still have so many of these to make. Perhaps if I showed you how, you could help?"

Blue eyes flashed and perfectly rosy lips pouted. "No, no. I have no talent for that."

No talent for folding paper? "It takes very little aptitude, I assure you. I will show you how and then you can follow me. We will get them done twice as fast."

Mrs. Burke fluttered her eyelashes at Wallace. "My aptitudes lie in other directions. I am sure I would just slow you down."

Charlotte took a deep breath, her fingers itching to rip her paper into tiny little shreds.

Four more days. Five at the most. She could make it. After three years of living here, she could handle five more days. If everything went according to Aunt Johanna's plan (which it always did), then her aunt would write a letter to Charlotte's mother saying Charlotte had proven herself respectable.

Five more days and she would be that much closer to packing her trunks and going home. Back to her siblings and her friends and freedom. Here she was essentially a lady's companion, scraping to do her aunt's bidding. At home, she could go back to laughing and leisure and little excursions to the shop.

Everything would go back to normal. To how it was before her shameful waltz.

The only thing that would remain the same was her vow to never be fooled by a man ever again. That one thing would remain rock solid.

Wallace didn't count. He was a cousin. And he was too boring to fool anyone.

Charlotte heard the arrival of a carriage and the usual sounds of doors opening and closing. She stood from the small table and, relieved to walk away from the dratted paper, excused herself from the salon.

The hall bustled. A footman held open the door, the butler greeted two newcomers, a maid stood out of the way and her aunt descended the stairs.

Her aunt's greeting echoed off the marble floor. "Oh, welcome! I am so glad you made good time."

A stout, elderly gentleman held his hat out for someone to take, as if things magically appeared and disappeared at his will, all he had to do was hold out his arm. A footman took his richly lined coat but the newcomer grasped his walking stick as if he would whack someone with it should they try to take it away.

He moved forward to greet his hostess and Charlotte blinked at the tiny figure who had been hidden behind the stout gentleman. A young woman handed her dashing hat to the footman and turned a shy, friendly smile on Charlotte.

She couldn't help but smile back.

The woman's father called her over, "Emma, Emma dear, come say hello."

Emma blushed and cast her eyes to the floor as she followed her father's bidding. Wallace had entered the hall and Aunt Johanna administered a round of introductions.

A small part of Charlotte wanted to squeeze the doll-like Emma in a hug and drag her around the house, showing her all the fun things they could now do.

So this was the young woman Aunt Johanna wanted her godson to marry. Her aunt planned to will most of her fortune to her godson, Henry Simmons. In exchange, she had certain expectations of him, including a proper marriage to a proper young lady.

And Emma was clearly everything proper.

Oh, this Christmas party would be splendid. Everything was falling into place. Charlotte would make her paper flowers. Henry would fall in love with the perfect English rose that was

Emma, and then at the end of everything, everyone would go home. Including Charlotte.

Chapter 2

There was something about freezing away all feeling that had appealed to him this morning. If he had been any less of a Corinthian, he would regret his decision, but the weather, although cold, was temporarily clear. That was all the sportsman in him could ask for.

He wasn't sure he had fingers or toes anymore, and even his riding cloak felt like it had frozen in place behind him. If only his ride had frozen his heart, too.

His crumbling estate needed to be updated and Blenworth House needed a new roof.

His own luck on the marriage mart had been unsuccessful. Certainly a gentleman with a fortune could find a wife with his eyes closed, but Henry had to rely on his good looks. Which didn't get him very far once a potential bride and her father realized the dreary state of his affairs.

He was tired of finding someone agreeable only to learn how materialistic she truly was when she turned on him. Ladies expected a certain minimum level of comfort that he couldn't guarantee. After all, a wife would only be so comfortable sitting under a leaky roof.

He needed an heiress. His pride told him he didn't want an heiress because he wanted the money. He told himself he would repair Blenworth House in time based on the amount of effort he put into his land. But he needed a wife who could comfortably support herself while waiting for his pride to catch up to her.

And, well, if her comfort included the purchase of a new roof, then so be it.

So here he was, answering the summons of his godmother who insisted Henry needed to marry. He agreed. He didn't mind starting a family. In fact, he looked forward to it. He wanted children to inherit his legacy.

But his godmother didn't have any wife in mind. She had an heiress. Her summons had been clear: Stay for a small Christmas party, meet an heiress, woo the heiress, and become engaged to said heiress.

Wincing as he dismounted, he then turned to grimace at his friend, who was chipper and red-cheeked. He called over the wind, "I'm going in."

The door blew open. No, that was a well-paid footman opening it. He wasn't used to such attentive staff.

He entered and sighed, the warm air stinging his cheeks back into feeling. He imagined he looked dreadful, his nose running, his face red, his eyes watering. All he wanted was to recuperate in whichever finely decorated room his godmother had chosen for him.

Johanna greeted him immediately. "Welcome, dear boy! You look like you rode past death and lived to tell us of it."

He smiled at her, or thought his frozen lips were smiling. Johanna was formidable but she meant well. She knew as well as he did that his estate had the capacity to be prosperous and that if his father hadn't gambled away the family fortune, Henry wouldn't be in these dire straits.

It took money to make money. It took money to care for tenant houses and divide pasture land and apply new planting techniques. Henry had a plan and he was slowly returning his inheritance back to what it had been. It didn't hurt that his godmother promised he was in her will.

He thought he felt a playful smack on his arm through his cloak but he was still thawing and couldn't be sure. He sniffled and responded, "Good to see you well." No less than four other people were staring at him and it nearly made him wish he had stayed with his horse. "My friend will be here in a moment for introductions."

Johanna waved away their audience. "Miss Moore, would you please show Miss Lawton her room?"

Two young women tore their gazes from him and blushed prettily. One of them, the prettier one, murmured something and turned to lead the way. Her thick blond hair piled behind her head in a way that was somehow ladylike and unruly, a few stray locks tumbling down past her slender neck. She had dark brows and lashes framing wide eyes, and a pert mouth, delicate and lusciously curved.

Johanna was saying something. "-like her very much."

She had said it quietly, just for him and he had no idea what she was talking about.

"I am happy to spend a pleasant Christmas with you, in particular."

She linked her arm through his and led him further into the hall. "I am glad. I-"

The door opened again. Henry stopped and grinned, thankful for the distraction from a loaded, rather dull conversation. "May I introduce my friend, Lord Sudbury. Sudbury, my one and only godmother, Mrs. Johanna Brancaster."

Sudbury smiled, bowed, and muttered the appropriate niceties but they all rolled off the old woman. Her lips pinched and he was certain the door was still open but it was actually a wave of fierce and chilling anger emanating from his godmother. She nodded her head once, crisply, and said, "I hadn't realized."

CHARLOTTE CLICKED THE door shut, leaving Emma to freshen up in her guest chamber.

A maid scurried down the hall. "There you are, miss. Your aunt wants you in the library right away."

No doubt, now that everyone was here, her aunt wanted to go over the plans for the evening and give Charlotte her role. If at all possible, they would need to occupy Mrs. Burke and keep her overt advances far away from cousin Wallace. If they could accomplish that, the night should go splendidly.

In the library, the sultry red drapes and dark wood shelving impressed a level of power that Aunt Johanna used to her advantage. All of her important meetings with staff were held here with Aunt Johanna strategically situated behind an imposing mahogany desk.

Charlotte entered and closed the heavy door behind her. Her aunt, who rarely drank, was pouring two snifters of brandy.

She hovered by the door and watched her aunt hand the second snifter to a man seated opposite the desk.

He turned to look at her, his eyes rimmed with dark lashes and, now that he wasn't so rosy from the cold, his tanned, chiseled cheeks cut down to a wide chin with a small cleft. Without his cloak, she could see broad shoulders and long arms, the snifter of brandy looking small and delicate in his large hands.

Aunt Johanna had indicated her godson was a bit of a Corinthian, but that meant little to Charlotte. Appropriate exercise for a lady meant a long walk or a chaperoned ride on her mare. But a man such as this one did not strain the fabric of his clothing by ladylike exercise. Indeed, following his finely tailored coat down from his shoulders, she couldn't help but wonder how the cut of his body resembled that of a marbled statue.

Aunt Johanna rolled her hand in the air. "Come in, have a seat. Miss Moore, please meet my godson, Mr. Henry Simmons. Henry, my niece, Miss Charlotte Moore. You two are here because we are in uncomfortable circumstances." She put her hand to her forehead and sighed. "We haven't even begun and things are already unraveling."

Henry smiled at her, his full lips widening in a way that suddenly chased the winter chill from the room.

She perched on the edge of a chair, her posture perfect and her hands clasped in her lap. Trying to focus on the matter at hand, she soothed, "Aunt Johanna, I hardly think anything so bad has happened already."

"Henry has invited a friend, something I gave him permission to do, thinking he would bring someone appropriate. We now have Lord Sudbury under our roof."

Her stomach dropped. Charlotte's hands clenched, twisting her striped muslin. "Surely not *the* Lord Sudbury."

Aunt Johanna scolded, "There is only one man with that title."

It would be too fortunate for her if that Lord Sudbury had, oh, died and let someone else inherit. No, no, no. Charlotte was careful around all men, but the one man whom she wished dreadful things upon, he was here.

Right now.

He had been invited to the party by Mr. Simmons. This man, the one she had been ogling a moment ago, this man cavorted around with the likes of Lord Sudbury, inviting the pest to Christmas parties.

She was standing and she wasn't even sure at what moment her body had moved. She demanded, "How could you bring that man?"

He coughed on his sip of brandy. "Pardon?"

She knew she was raising her voice, but the anger swelling through her needed an outlet. "You're friends with that man? Do you have any idea what-"

Her aunt interrupted, "Charlotte. I fully understand what you are feeling and you are validated for feeling that way. Now, please clam it all up like a proper Englishwoman and get yourself under control."

She sat again, the chair creaking when her weight dropped onto it. Closing her eyes, she took a deep breath. Three years ago, almost to the day, Lord Sudbury had caught her eye. He had looked like a chiseled statue and he had warmed the room when he smiled at her.

It had all been a sham. The man was a sham and Charlotte had spent the last three years in exile because of his joke. And now he had the audacity to even breathe under the same roof as her?

What gave him that right?

Mr. Simmons cleared his throat. "I am not sure why I feel the need to be apologetic? Perhaps I can somehow explain myself if I were to be told of the problem."

Aunt Johanna took another sip of brandy. "Miss Moore is here with me because Lord Sudbury behaved ungentlemanly to her in her home village. I am flabbergasted as to how you could associate with someone so lacking in morals and character."

Charlotte breathed in, not realizing her chest had felt so tight until it finally relaxed. Her aunt, for as domineering as the woman could be, was on Charlotte's side.

Mr. Simmons turned to face her directly, his stare pulling her gaze over to meet his. The spot between his eyebrows crinkled and his eyes, a warm brown, locked onto her. She felt a little heat rise up her neck and quickly broke the contact, looking down at her hands.

He said, "I had no idea. I see how this is a very uncomfortable situation indeed. May I ask what he did?"

She opened her mouth to answer but her aunt beat her to it. "He waltzed with her at a Christmas assembly before she had permission. Everyone in her acquaintance saw it and the next morning she was sent here to avoid any further embarrassment."

His voice sharp, he said, "But she went along with the waltz. How was he to know she didn't have permission?"

She was on her feet again, pointing at him, all of her anger directed at the insensitive pile of man. "He knew! He behaved as a rake of the worst kind and when it was all done, he merely smirked like it was all a joke. I was a joke to him. Do you have any idea..."

Her voice trailed off, giving way to a sob.

He looked away from her, his response so placid that her fingers twitched. She had to squash the sudden desire to launch at him and smack those chiseled cheeks. See how placid he could be then.

She just didn't want to be the only one in the room in pain.

Slowly, she sat again, staring at the faded red carpet.

Her aunt, proper, composed Englishwoman that she was, raised a brow. "I am not happy, Henry."

Aunt Johanna's ability to instill sense into absolutely anyone felt like a tiny ray of light through the gathering storm. Mr. Simmons stilled in his chair and it was rather satisfying to notice his grip tighten on his glass.

Her aunt continued, "My numbers for the party are already uneven and I can't let you make things worse. My true plans, let's not pretend, are not yet ruined. You must be here. However I am not beyond threatening Sudbury if he steps out of line. Can you convey that to him?"

Charlotte exploded, "You'll let him stay?"

She couldn't do this. She couldn't pretend to behave for that scoundrel.

Mr. Simmons, the deep even tone of his voice an affront to her senses, said, "Miss Moore, I give my word that Sudbury will behave and apologize. I am sorry that this misunderstanding has upended your life to such an extent."

Upended her life? Apologizing for the last three years was like wrapping a festering wound in a thin strip of gauze.

He had no idea. And how could he? He was a man, free to run amok, ruining lives as he saw fit because he was a mighty landowner. The world was his oyster.

But he was sorry. He, as a man, would make sure everything was okay. And she was supposed to trust that?

But she couldn't. She couldn't trust him as far as she could throw his muscled bulk.

He was sorry.

He was worthless.

More of her aunt's independent attitude must have rubbed off on her than Charlotte had realized. Her mother would be scandalized to know her thoughts right now. Questioning a man's judgment.

But what else could she do?

Try as she might, she couldn't accept that this situation was her fault.

The wind battered against the window.

Her aunt was going to let Lord Sudbury stay.

This Christmas party wasn't going to be as easy as she had thought.

Chapter 3

His godmother wasted no time in leaving him alone with Miss Emma Lawton, claiming she needed to speak with the elder Mrs. Burke.

He stood near the windows with Miss Lawton, purposefully situated in a location in the drawing room that allowed for a semi-private conversation.

He couldn't say his godmother hadn't chosen well. Miss Lawton was as beautiful as an English rose, blond hair neatly coiffed, her rosy dress of fine fabric complimenting the small blush hiding behind her porcelain skin.

He smiled at her, feeling the tight pull of his lips and wishing he could manage something more genuine. "I hear you are a neighbor of Mrs. Brancaster's. Do you visit here often?"

She toyed with a tassel and said, "Oh, no. Not often."

He tried again. "Your father and Mrs. Brancaster appear to be good friends."

She still didn't look at him when she responded, "Yes, I think they have known each other a long time."

Well, this conversation was titillating. Henry tried not to roll his eyes, not that Miss Lawton would see the gesture since she wasn't looking at him.

He switched tactics. "I had a long ride here, myself. Do you enjoy riding?"

"No, not really."

Swell.

"Are you looking forward to dinner? I hear my godmother has an excellent cook."

"Yes, of course."

"I am partial to a warm soup in weather such as this."

"And I as well."

"Is there a flavor you prefer?"

He couldn't believe Miss Lawton couldn't hear his teeth grinding. Or maybe she could. He clenched his hands behind his back and nodded at Miss Moore as she glided over.

She slipped her arm through Miss Lawton's. "That pink is a splendid color on you. I can't wait to see your Christmas dress."

Miss Lawton blushed and smiled prettily.

Miss Moore continued, "Mr. Simmons, Miss Lawton was so helpful this afternoon with the decorations. We finished folding all the paper and, thanks to her, we will be able to finish decorating tomorrow."

Was Miss Moore trying to help him woo the heiress? This Miss Moore was very different from the one he had met earlier. She looked the same, but she somehow also looked better?

Of course she did. She was dressed for the evening in an ivory gown with a small amount of gold embroidery. The warmth of the gold matched how the light played in her hair. Something in her simmered with an energy that drew him in and he had to remind himself that he was here for someone else.

Miss Lawton managed a decent response. "I do think the house will look lovely tomorrow."

At least the woman could, eventually, formulate a complete sentence. And it included her opinion at that.

Miss Moore said, "For all of our effort, I hope I can convince my aunt to keep the paper roses until next year. As pretty as they are, I cannot say I want to make them all over again."

Miss Lawton smiled, dropping her tassel. "I am glad I learned how to make them. I actually look forward to crafting more next year."

Miss Moore opened her mouth to respond but he cut her off, hoping to redirect the conversation. "I am now looking forward to seeing these roses. I imagine I can help hang them wherever you ladies prefer."

Miss Moore's eyes swept up to meet his. They sparked for just a moment before reverting back to Miss Lawton.

What had she just been thinking?

Suddenly, her eyes whipped to the door and she stood a little straighter, her arm tightening around Miss Lawton's.

He smiled and nodded at Sudbury, then turned back to the ladies. Miss Moore stared at the wall, looking in the opposite direction, and he swore he saw her lower lip tremble. She blinked a few times, only turning, stone-faced, once Sudbury joined them.

Henry said. "I believe you were all introduced earlier."

Since Miss Moore looked a little as if she had sucked on a lemon, Henry wasn't surprised when his friend focused his attention on Miss Lawton.

Sudbury said, "I am so glad we made it here before the wind picked up and now that I am here, I am ready for the festivities. I think, above all, I am ready for some music."

At that, Miss Lawton's eyes lit with interest and Henry had to tamp down a bout of jealousy. Sudbury had a way with women and how he had known Miss Lawton would like music was a mystery to Henry.

Miss Lawton smiled wide, her entire face glowing with delight. "There is a collection of music over by the pianoforte. Would you care to peruse the sheets with me?"

They turned and Sudbury led away the woman Henry's godmother wanted him to marry.

This first meeting could have gone worse, but not by much.

He had forgotten Miss Moore until she puffed out a frustrated breath. Her brows were scrunched as she, too, watched the couple walk away.

He said, "I suppose that did not go according to plan."

Her voice tight, she said, "Nothing about this holiday is going according to plan."

She turned to look up at him, some of the tension easing from her face. His godmother was her aunt and, even though they didn't know each other, they knew how much Johanna liked her plans. It was odd to think he shared something so knowing with a stranger.

He said, "Miss Moore, I am sorry we met under less than ideal circumstances. I am having difficulty casting the person I see now against the one I met a few hours ago."

The shadow of frustration fell back over her features and she twisted her gloved fingers together. "I suppose you have met Miss Lawton under more desirable circumstances and that must count for something. I think Aunt Johanna did say that Miss Lawton had a nice singing voice so I am not surprised at her enthusiasm. I believe she is also accomplished in embroidery and can speak fluent French."

He smirked, "Can't most women claim similar accomplishments?"

"I do not speak French."

She was quick to admit that. He asked, "*Vous ne parlez pas francais?*"

"I can, Mr. Simmons, understand that much. But this isn't about me."

"Isn't it?"

"No. This is about you and Miss Lawton." She sighed. "All part of Aunt Johanna's plan."

"Speaking of plans, what is for dinner?"

"I think a remove of *soupe de chou-fleur au zest d'orange*, then you may like *boeuf bourguignon*, and likely the *crepes aux pommes et au calvados*."

He smiled at her. "Interesting. I thought you did not speak French.

She flipped her hand in the air. "If you know your way through a dinner menu, then that is all the French you need to know. I didn't have the patience to learn any more than that."

She was a little nonchalant about all the years he had spent mastering French. "I suppose you were busy studying other things."

She smiled back up at him, her eyes catching that sparkle he had noticed a few minutes ago. Or maybe it was the candlelight catching her just right. Something shimmered behind the gray, setting her gaze to an intriguing silver and he realized he had dipped his head closer to hers.

She cleared her throat and looked away at the same moment he did.

She said, "Since she is fluent in the language, Miss Lawton is a shining example of what a wife should be."

If he could get Miss Lawton to tell him anything, other than that she liked soup, he may be able to agree with Miss Moore. He could admit that Miss Lawton was pretty, but what else had his godmother seen in the girl that he was missing?

Was it just him? She had been able to converse with Sudbury. He would have to speak with his godmother. He wanted to trust her judgment and at this point he didn't trust his own.

Any heiress would do.

He followed Miss Moore's gaze straight over to Sudbury. "You don't trust her with him."

"I don't trust any woman with that rake."

"Those are harsh words. This is a rather public setting. I doubt anything untoward could happen here."

She turned her face up to him, but this time, her eyes burned, glaring at him with a ferocity he hadn't expected. She said, "I was in a very public place when he ruined my reputation. It makes no difference to a man like him."

She couldn't lay the blame entirely at one man's door. "It takes two to waltz, Miss Moore."

She stepped away, her eyes blazing in a way that felt like sharp talons, her scorn like a scratch against his polished exterior.

He would never know what her response would have been because just then the butler announced dinner.

Chapter 4

Around this time of year, the breakfast parlor smelled of pork. Aunt Johanna also had eggs or, for the dainty ladies, plenty of toast.

Charlotte couldn't eat anything until she had first partaken of a cup of morning tea. Winter brought dreadfully dry air and she woke each morning feeling the need to hydrate with something warm. Next to her, Mrs. Katherine Burke took a delicate nibble of toast and both ladies ignored the mountain of meat on Wallace's plate.

Who had decided ladies should only eat toast in the morning? Why, when there were so many other things that smelled and tasted so much more wholesome, were ladies relegated to something so boring?

She muttered, "Maybe I will have eggs this morning."

Next to her, Mrs. Burke hummed through her bite. "Mr. Burke used to eat quite a few every morning. Or kippers. He swore kippers were," she paused and stared at her tea, "the key to health."

Mrs. Burke was technically out of mourning but she still wore a long-sleeved, lavender dress. Charlotte asked, "Do you miss him?"

"Every day."

In the quiet, Charlotte took another sip of her tea, the beverage soothing her dry throat. She didn't think someone like Mrs. Burke would have cared for her husband, especially considering the way the woman threw herself at cousin Wallace.

Mrs. Burke said, "I hear we are going shopping today."

Shopping! "We are! Every year Aunt Johanna donates new items to the church. I have a list of a few things the parish has requested."

"I haven't been shopping in a while and want to see what the shops have to offer. Is there anywhere you care to visit, Miss Moore?"

With what money? Charlotte had been sent off in disgrace. It wasn't as if her family sent her pin money. Would she like to peruse all the shops and spoil herself a little? Yes. But Aunt Johanna would only give her money for things on the list and would likely request receipts for all purchases.

"I am afraid I will be occupied purchasing the things on the parish's list."

Wallace was mid-bite when Mrs. Burke redirected her attention to him. "Are you coming as well?"

Charlotte turned away to roll her eyes, trying to hide her expression behind her cup. Mrs. Burke had sunk her talons into Wallace and wasn't going to let go easily.

And to think for a moment she had felt sorry for the widow.

Once again, Charlotte found herself wishing these days would pass quickly. Tomorrow was Christmas Eve and, despite the feelings normally associated with the holiday, this year filled her with more dread than usual.

SHE FINGERED A PAIR of luxuriously soft, white gloves. She squashed the urge to try them on and focused on the pairs of knitted mittens.

Her list said to buy five pairs, but for whose hands? Children? Women? Men? Mittens were no use unless they fit.

The bell jangled and with a frigid gust, Mrs. Burke entered, lowering her fur-lined hood. Her eyes settled immediately upon Charlotte and she smiled, ignoring the clerk completely. "I have just come from Mr. Brooks's and I must say the shop is splendid. I don't suppose your cousin has a favorite flower."

"Cousin Wallace?"

"Of course." In a rather bold and intimate maneuver, she wound her arm under Charlotte's elbow. "Do you have any tips? Anything I can do to win him over?"

Charlotte blinked. She desperately wished she had a more intelligent response than a blank stare.

"He is technically not even a blood relation to you. I am surprised that after all this time, you haven't caught his attention. You are very pretty, Charlotte. May I call you Charlotte? You must call me Katherine as Mrs. Burke is my mother by marriage."

A little smile tugged at the corners of her lips. "Of course. As to cousin Wallace, I don't think our personalities are quite suited for each other."

Katherine patted her arm. "That makes sense. Mr. Burke fit into my life in such a way that, you could say, we were made for each other. When someone else settles so comfortably into the way you do things, before you know it, you're doing all these things together but it barely feels like anything has changed. Yet, everything has changed."

Charlotte nodded along as if Katherine's ramblings made sense. She avoided looking at those pristine, white gloves on the table and focused on a shelf. She needed five pairs of stockings for donation but, again, had no sizes. She would have to do her best. "I am very sorry for your loss, Katherine."

The widow had gone quiet. When Charlotte looked up, Katherine was staring, seeming to see nothing at all. Suddenly she exclaimed, "Oh, isn't that green just the color for Christmas?"

Charlotte sighed. Maybe Aunt Johanna wouldn't mind if Charlotte made a purchase for herself. She couldn't afford the gloves, but Mr. Cole's Library wasn't far and she doubted any of the other guests would be there, which made the excursion that much more appealing.

Katherine said, "It would match the emeralds I brought with me."

Charlotte nodded. "The ones you wore last night."

"Yes. They were a gift from Mr. Burke."

Charlotte bit her lip at the haunted expression in Katherine's eyes. The widow asked, "Would you mind if I accompany you around for the rest of your shopping?"

It would be rude to say no, wouldn't it? "Of course." She held up her selections. "Allow me a moment to bring these to the clerk."

While the young man tallied the items and wrote out a receipt, the door jangled again, opening with another burst of frigid air.

A petite voice trilled, "Charlotte, there you are!"

"Emma! Oh, and Mr. Simmons is with you."

Good. At least one of her aunt's plans was working. The more that went her aunt's way, the sooner Charlotte could go home.

Mr. Simmons stepped inside and quickly closed the door behind him, shutting out the freezing air. His eyes quickly roamed the shop before lowering to settle on her. Last night, she hadn't realized how tall he was, but now that his form filled the doorway, his height struck her. She had to lift her gaze to his, returning his greeting.

His wide smile settled handsomely across his features and she paused, suspicious of his easy manners.

She held up her packages. "I was just leaving."

Emma called her. "Wait! Charlotte, what do you think of this color?"

Mr. Simmons quietly extended his hand. He had long fingers and she realized she was staring.

He said, "May I hold that for you?"

She passed over the package, blushing. "Of course. Thank you."

Maybe it had been too long since she had allowed herself to find a man attractive. She quickly turned away to see what Emma needed.

Emma held up the deep green shawl of soft cashmere. "Do you not think this would complement Mrs. Burke's emeralds?" She held up the fabric to Katherine's shoulder. "It would suit perfectly."

Katherine blushed and tried to push away the shawl. "It is lovely of you to think of me. I had thought the shawl the perfect color as well."

Emma wouldn't let go of the fabric. "Then you must buy it!"

Katherine stuttered. "Oh, n-no. I really couldn't. You see, well..."

The clerk cleared his throat, breaking the awkward silence.

Charlotte stepped forward, taking the shawl and folding it up. She felt guilty for lying to someone as kind as Emma but couldn't stand to let the moment linger. "It is such fine fabric; however, Mrs. Burke forgot her pin money back at the house."

Katherine's eyes widened but she nodded along. "Yes, so silly of me."

Emma grinned. "Oh, well then I can purchase it and you can pay me back when we return."

Katherine sucked in a deep breath and speared Charlotte with imploring eyes. Why was Charlotte always finding herself entangled in these strange situations?

Katherine patted her hand on the shawl. "You know, I have a shawl near this shade that I forgot at home. I think I will just have to pass on this one as I do not need two."

Emma laughed. "Oh, I could argue that point!"

While Katherine listened to Emma ramble, Charlotte glanced over at the gloves she would never buy.

Mr. Simmons caught the direction of her gaze. "Have you tried them on?"

"No. I don't need them and have other errands, yet."

Something flickered in his expression but he simply murmured, "Very practical of you."

She changed the subject. "Have you found anything for donation?"

He smiled, a layer of charm and a little twinkle of mischief in his eyes. "I am taking the gentlemanly way out and simply donating my money. The parish can do what they will with it."

"I suppose that is also practical. I think if Aunt Johanna didn't have me, she would do the same."

"I have to disagree with you. My gesture is rather lazy and my godmother prefers to know her money is being put to good use. She would rather donate the mittens needed," he patted the package, "than leave her money open to someone's ill judgment."

She laughed, enjoying their camaraderie. "You know my aunt rather well, Mr. Simmons!"

He chuckled, too. "I do. I am surprised after all these years that I haven't met you."

She held her hand out for the package. "Alas, it likely wasn't in my aunt's plan. I was supposed to be hiding away, thinking over my shame. Not at all a state suitable for meeting…"

Her voice trailed off as she struggled to avoid the words she had wanted to say. That she wasn't supposed to be meeting handsome men.

He tapped his fingers against her package and leaned over conspiratorially. "Now I must know how you were going to finish that sentence."

She pursed her lips, making a point of remaining silent.

He sighed, an exaggerated, defeated sound. "Fine. But you are wrong again, anyway. My aunt wouldn't ask you to spend three years in a state of shame."

"She has not asked that of me. My family has, by denying my return home. Aunt Johanna has promised to send me home after the Christmas party."

"So much at stake at one little Christmas celebration."

"How very accurate of you to notice. I am here for my home and you are here for love."

His eyes clouded and he stepped back. "I wouldn't say that."

His sudden change affected her, a dull disappointment tugging away her humor. She looked away and caustically taunted, "Not a believer in love?"

"No."

He said it so vehemently. As a handsome, charming man, he probably didn't think it fashionable to believe in love.

The bell over the door jangled and Lord Sudbury entered, accompanied by a cold gust of wind.

She held her hand out for her package again.

Mr. Simmons tapped his fingers on it. "I did not mean to dampen our good mood."

She quietly waggled her fingers at him, purposefully avoiding looking at Lord Sudbury.

He handed the package over. "I will see you after dinner, though."

She gestured over to Emma, reminding him of Aunt Johanna's plans. "Until then, Mr. Simmons."

Chapter 5

Tomorrow would be Christmas Eve. The sooner it was here, the sooner it could go.

Charlotte listened to a mish-mash of poetry. The words selected for their game were difficult but Emma, dressed tonight in a gown of celestial blue and lace, trudged through her poem in high spirit.

"There once was a cat called Trouble,
Who walked with a funny canter.
He lived in his own little bubble,
But could catch mice on the double
And left them no room for banter."

Lord Sudbury was the first to clap and congratulate Emma on a spirited story. Mr. Simmons should be the one fawning over her, but Charlotte was a little relieved to see him as quiet as she was.

Aunt Johanna, sitting between the elder Mrs. Burke and Mr. Simmons, nudged the latter to join Lord Sudbury in offering his admiration. Her aunt hadn't spent the day shopping so she could not have known how bored Mr. Simmons was around Emma. He put in a good effort to engage her in conversation, to elicit any kind of opinion or comment, and spent most of the day trying to dote on the woman his godmother wanted him to marry. He had truly tried. He had held packages, doors, and on many occasions, Charlotte was amused to see him hold his tongue.

So far, the courtship was not going well.

Aunt Johanna nodded with a tight-lipped smile and then quickly turned her attention to Charlotte, her focus like that of a falcon. "Why don't you read your rhymes, now?"

Her aunt had phrased it like a question.

Charlotte crinkled her paper between gloved fingers.

It wasn't really a question.

She cleared her throat. "Of course."

She cleared her throat again. She shouldn't have been so harsh on Emma. At least she had looked pretty, with the firelight catching in her curls and her sweet voice softening the blunt rhymes.

Charlotte could do this. In front of everyone. It was her own suggestion that they play this game.

Her eyes flicked to Mr. Simmons. He stared, waiting, and she couldn't decide if that made her feel better or worse.

She crinkled her paper again in her lap.

Mr. Simmons drew everyone's attention to him. "Actually, I am prepared to read mine, if Miss Moore doesn't mind waiting."

She smiled, the gesture mirroring the relief she felt in the rest of her body as her tension eased. "Thank you, Mr. Simmons. I would love to hear your rhymes."

He flicked the paper with his finger and stood.

"He rode with two pistols and his trouble.

But his stubborn horse refused to canter.

His anger began to bubble.

'Go, you beast, on the double!'

The roan snickered, she lived for the banter."

Lord Sudbury laughed. "Oh, yours is much more clever than mine!"

Mr. Simmons said, "I had a horse in mind when I wrote this. Do you remember Guinevere?"

"That pretty roan with a temper?"

"Just the one!"

The room listened while Mr. Simmons and Lord Sudbury told a rather ribald story of something to do with his roan Guinevere, a stile, and a rowdy chase. After, his eyes sparkling with good humor, he turned to Charlotte and said, "Did you not say you had prepared charades?"

Grateful for her ability to multitask, she smiled and answered him while also hiding her paper. Mr. Simmons had successfully diverted everyone's attention from her rhymes and she was grateful to play along. "Yes, of course. I have a stack of prepared items. Do we want to play in teams?"

When she prepared the game, in the spirit of the holiday, she had tried to think of things related to Christmas. She wasn't sure how someone would act out a yule log, but that was for the unlucky person who drew the item to worry about. She hoped they held their arms stiff and hilariously rolled around on the floor like a log.

On her own turn, she blinked at her item.

Yule log.

Of course this was the one she picked. She sighed, folded the paper back in half, and held up two fingers.

Katherine said, "Two words."

Charlotte nodded and looked at the empty space around her. Good grief.

Mr. Simmons, with his fob watch out, kept time. She tried not to look at him, feeling a flush creep up her cheeks already. Her team needed a win and she wasn't going to let them down.

The game of charades was war and it was ladies against the men. Failure was not an option.

She drew a large square around her with her arms and then pretended to tend a fire.

Charlotte wasted a moment staring in surprise when Emma yelled, "Fireplace!"

She nodded and waved her arm to suggest she had more. She pretended to drag something large over to her newly imagined fireplace and pretended to inspect the end of the large thing before heaving it into the fire.

"Chopped wood!"

She pretended to start a fire.

"Warm fire!"

"Chestnuts?"

Mr. Simmons pointed at his fob watch.

"Wood log!"

Charlotte stopped and pointed at Katherine.

"Wood log? Wood stick? Christmas, Christmas, Christmas. Yule log!"

Charlotte nodded and squealed.

"Yule log! We got it!"

Katherine laughed. "You are quite the actress, Miss Moore."

The women were winning, but if the men won this round, they would be tied.

Mr. Simmons stood, looked at his paper, and slumped his wide shoulders. He looked up at his audience with a tight expression, handed his watch to his godmother, and nodded.

He took a breath. He scrunched his brows. Charlotte stifled a giggle. She pressed her fingers to her lips. What word could he have that was so bad? After all, she had acted out a yule log.

He held up one finger.

"One word."

Cradling his arms together, he rocked them back and forth.

"Baby!"

"Jesus!"

"Baby Jesus!"

"Christ."

Charlotte was glad her lips were pressed to her mouth, her breath hitching. He held his long arms so gracefully, a perfect cradle to protect a tiny infant. But it wasn't just the way he held his arms, it was the way he looked down at a pretend infant and his eyelids fluttered.

For just a moment, she caught a sense of tenderness before he turned to the side and pretended to set the imaginary baby down. Then he stood back and drew a long rectangle around the area he had just set the baby.

"Cot?"

"Bed!"

Manger. He had set the baby in the manger. From the tension flowing through her teammates, it felt like she wasn't the only one to guess the word.

Aunt Johanna held up the watch. The men were running out of time.

Mr. Simmons rubbed his hand down his face. He pretended to pour something over the spot he had just set the baby and a few giggles escaped when he bent over and pretended to open his mouth and gobble up something imaginary.

"Good God, man, are you eating the baby?"

Aunt Johanna called time. Charlotte and her team burst into laughter.

Mr. Simmons straightened, glaring at his team. "Manger! The word was manger."

There was a collective sound of understanding from the men as they all realized Mr. Simmons had not been eating the baby. He had been pouring feed into the manger and was pretending to be an animal eating it.

Charlotte grinned. It was fun winning.

Everyone exchanged their personal congratulations. Charlotte turned from her cousin to stare into a familiar pair of green eyes.

She dipped into a shallow curtsy. "Lord Sudbury. Good game."

Turning again to show him her shoulder, she cringed at the gloved fingers on her arm. "Miss Moore. Your performance was brilliant. You had a difficult word but pulled through for your team. Very admirable."

If she didn't know those soft green eyes belonged to a practiced liar, she would believe his flummery.

The hand hadn't left her arm. "Henry has told me that I must have a private word with you."

She had no interest in being alone with him and deflected, "Perhaps we will find a moment tomorrow."

He smiled and nodded, turning to congratulate Katherine.

She didn't want to talk to the man. Oh, there were many things she wanted to do to him, but none of them involved talking.

Mr. Simmons was next to congratulate her. How could two men who were supposedly friends be so different?

Or were they?

Chapter 6

Aunt Johanna had given her a list of items to check before bed. Charlotte sneaked in a little remark about how she had everything in order, but Aunt Johanna brushed her off with a regal wave of her hand.

For tomorrow, Hobson had sworn the cold winds of today would blow on through. If it was calmer and there was a layer of cloud cover, it could be a nice day for skating. That meant the skates should be brought down from the attic and cleaned.

Then, not that Aunt Johanna didn't trust the kitchen, but she specifically didn't want to leave things to chance, so Charlotte had to check the progress of the cake.

Her dry eyes were beyond the salvation of blinking. Tomorrow would be an even longer day, as it was Christmas Eve. She had to organize the possible skating excursion to the lake and if the weather wasn't agreeable, she had indoor activities planned. Later, everyone would hang up the greenery and she still had to plan supper and check with the kitchen about tea.

If the holiday was an incoming storm, tomorrow was black clouds rolling in.

She ran her finger over the side of a skate. They were ready for tomorrow.

If she had to be honest with herself, the games tonight had been fun. She couldn't remember the last time she had laughed with people near her own age. She had been cooped up with her aunt for so long that it felt good to remember that there was an upside to all the work going into her preparations.

Tonight had been a taste of the fun she used to have back home, the games she used to play with her friends and family. In three days, she resolved to pack her trunks with everyone else. If following the boring rules of society meant that she could go back to interacting with people her own age, then that is what she would do.

She was ready and all she had to do was prove it to her aunt.

That night so long ago still stood out in her mind as a crystal clear memory. The shocked expressions and snickers of the townsfolk. The snide look from Sudbury after the waltz. The reprimanding tone of her mother's voice.

The shame that had sunk into her stomach.

These three years with her aunt had dulled the embarrassment, though. She remembered the feelings, but she thought she was ready to move past them. She didn't want this hanging over her life anymore.

Her candle flickered down the dark hall and she was surprised to see a glow ahead of her in the kitchen.

She wavered for a moment, not wanting to intrude. But it would only take her a moment to check the cake and the servants all knew she wouldn't bother them. Or tell her aunt.

Four men stood around a shallow dish on the end of the table. She immediately recognized two footmen and the other two, having cast off their jackets, stumped her.

Was that Mr. Simmons?

The sleeves of his white shirt were rolled up to his elbows and without his jacket, she could see how his back triangulated from his wide shoulders down to his athletic waist, his pantaloons snug over...

Her cheeks heated and she quickly looked away.

Lord Sudbury was here, too.

Judd, one of the footmen, saw her first. "Miss Moore!"

All four men turned to her. "I was only checking on the fruit. Family recipe, you know."

Lord Sudbury smiled his familiar predatory grin. The kind of smile that was meant to disarm but only put her on edge. "Join us? We are starting a game of snapdragon."

Part of her wanted to admonish them for playing something so dangerous. But another part of her, a reckless part of her that she had spent the last three years tamping down because it only ever brought her trouble, wanted to join them. "Is that why you are down here so late and in the dark?"

The footmen exchanged nervous glances but Mr. Simmons waved her over. "You don't have to play, but you can watch if you would like. It is fun."

The consequences would be disastrous if she was caught.

She had never played the game before. The little fiery voice down in her heart told her that the least she could do was watch.

She swayed, torn between leaving the kitchen or joining the men, unchaperoned, to watch a game that literally played with fire.

It would be fun.

The charades had been amusing. It had felt so good to feel her body uncoil, letting the laughter relax her constant state of tension. She had to find a balance between having fun and following the rules.

She stepped up to the table, setting down her candle. "Okay. I'll watch a round."

The men relaxed and grinned. Judd sprinkled raisins into the dish.

Lord Sudbury asked, "Ready?"

Everyone nodded, he struck a match, and the bowl erupted in ghostly blue flame, illuminating their faces with an ominous pallor. Sparks of orange flared as the fire danced back and forth on the plate.

Charlotte watched, her mouth admittedly hanging open and a gasp of shock erupting from her mouth, as Judd snatched out a raisin. "Are you not burned?"

He grinned and popped the raisin into his mouth.

The men took turns snatching out raisins and Charlotte inched closer, completely mesmerized by the sway of the fire. The men didn't seem to mind at all what they were doing. They laughed and grinned and joked about it, teasing Judd when he pulled his hand back from a lick of orange.

Mr. Simmons turned to her and winked, his features sharp against the glow. "The blue is fine. It's the flashes of orange you have to watch out for."

As the fire died, the flame burned back and forth over the plate, at which point the men snatched out raisins faster than ever, not even taking turns. When it was all done, Charlotte realized she needed to take a deep breath of relief.

"You are all truly unhurt?"

Mr. Simmons smiled. "Truly. Would you like to try?"

She stepped back. "Oh, I don't think I should."

But there was that little spark inside her, telling her to try it.

Lord Sudbury laughed a pitch too high. "She's a proper lady, not interested in our games."

Her hair raised on her arms and she clenched her fists, gasping. His taunt struck at a chord inside of her that felt out of tune. She was interested in the game, but he was right that a proper lady would not be.

She sucked in a deep breath. She had just resolved to behave like a proper lady so she could go home, yet here she was breaking the rules again. What was wrong with her?

She ignored everyone else in the room as she whirled around and fled.

THE ROOM WAS QUITE a few degrees chillier than it had been a moment ago and it had nothing to do with the fire that had just gone out.

It was likely too dark for him to see it, but Henry directed a glare at Sudbury. His friend had claimed he didn't remember Miss Moore at all. Henry wasn't sure how to proceed with that information, considering how much Miss Moore's life had changed, and she claimed it was because of Sudbury. How could reparations move forward if one party didn't know they had caused any damage?

The brandy was not only in the dish, the men had imbibed a fair amount themselves. Sudbury wasn't always the nicest drunk. He probably didn't realize he had hurt Miss Moore. Instead, he was eating the rest of the brandy-soaked raisins and asking about another round.

Henry shook his head and looked at the doorway. "I will return in a moment."

He caught Miss Moore on the stairs and boldly grabbed her hand to stop her. "Wait."

In the flickering light of her candle, he could see her raised brows, her mouth still set in anger.

He said, "I did speak with Sudbury."

"Yes. He asked to have a private word with me. Something I am not in a hurry to do."

He stepped up another step, closer to her. Her features relaxed and, when he was a step down from her, they were at eye level. Equal. "He is not on his best behavior when he drinks."

"I am tired, Mr. Simmons."

They were alone in a dark hallway after most of the household had gone to bed. The moment felt just as comfortable as it did scandalous. He should let her go, let propriety guide his actions.

She was so pretty. Her shawl wrapped around her shoulders and delicate, bare fingers clutched the ends together. Tendrils of hair were coming undone and falling down her neck. Her hair always looked as if it was the pull of a pin away from tumbling free. For as proper as she behaved, everything else about her, her hair, her excitable eyes, the rampant sound of her laughter, said there was something more under her surface.

Underneath the layer of the lady.

She stared at him, at eye level, those wide eyes searching his. While he had been thinking about her, she had leaned forward.

"Mr. Simmons?"

Her breathy voice was the only sound in the silent stairway. They were utterly alone.

Her gaze shifted to his lips and in his peripheral vision, he saw her chest rise and fall with a heavy breath. He inched closer, smelling the slightest hint of sweet musk. The scent of her. Was it from her hair? A perfume?

If he nosed around, over her neck, up past her ear, he could figure that out.

He was close enough, he tilted his head and dragged the tip of his nose under her ear, breathing her in. Her own breath hitched and she said his name again. "Mr. Simmons."

In the chilly hallway, he could feel the heat of her next to him like the welcoming warmth of a hearth. He wrapped a hand around her waist, just under her shawl, over the soft satin of her evening gown.

She turned her head to meet his and their lips brushed. Her eyes were closed and her features softened. Now she looked like a woman who wanted to be kissed.

Just as he pressed his lips closer, her eyes opened and she pulled back. Something flashed and her brows dropped in anger, a pucker forming between them. She turned away so fast her candle flickered and nearly went out. In a moment, she was gone, leaving him alone on the stairs.

Chapter 7

She took her first slippery step onto the ice. The last time she had skated was with her sisters. There was something graceful and freeing about gliding about, moving in a way and at a speed she couldn't accomplish on her own two feet without the skates. The frigid December air whipped past her face as she sped off to the other side, leaving all the guests behind.

She raced off, enjoying the exhilaration of frigid air whizzing past her chilly cheeks while she skimmed over the frozen ice. It felt like flying.

It felt freeing.

It made her soul sing.

Her thoughts of Mr. Simmons were enough to keep her warm. The man himself radiated a kind of heat that drew her to him, like that of a hearth. Last night, he had wrapped an arm around her, enveloping her in his warmth. He even smelled warm, like a soft hint of spice and, oh, she didn't know, but she would call it the scent of a *man*.

Mr. Simmons had a specific musk to him that mingled with his skin and gave him a tempting essence.

Too tempting.

They had nearly kissed on the stairs.

She wanted to be so angry at him for taking advantage of her on a dark stairwell, but she really had no one to blame but herself because she knew better. She knew the men Mr. Simmons called his friends and she shouldn't expect anything other than rakish behavior from him.

Not to mention that Mr. Simmons was here to become engaged to someone else. It wasn't an arranged marriage, per sé, but Aunt Johanna did not sound like she left a lot of wiggle room in the matter.

She knew her aunt planned to will her fortune to Mr. Simmons. She knew he needed the funds. And, she knew as well as he did, that he needed an heiress like Emma. He had already decided he wouldn't marry for love and for a man in his position, that made sense.

What didn't make sense was why Mr. Simmons would risk everything for one little kiss from her.

It probably would have been a magnificent kiss.

Charlotte spun on the ice and sighed, throwing her arms out for balance. Why were rakes her weakness?

What about her made men think it was okay to toy with her feelings? She knew better than to trust a handsome smile.

All the more reason to stay away from Mr. Simmons.

She heard the scrape of skates behind her. Coming her way was the other man she wanted to avoid. "Lord Sudbury."

His hat shadowed his eyes, but he smiled softly. As he drew nearer, she could see his strained look of apprehension. "Miss Moore. I have come to speak with you. And apologize."

She straightened and stood still, her foot at an angle to steady her on the skates. "I see."

He waved his hand back at the other guests still on the far side of the lake. "I think this counts as a rather private conversation."

She nodded. No one could overhear them, but everyone could see them. "Yes."

He took a deep breath and straightened his jacket over his chest. "I, er, I am ashamed to say I was a spoiled brat before I met Mr. Simmons. And it sounds as if you were a recipient of my, well, rottenness."

"It was rather rotten, what you did."

"Would you elaborate on what it was that I did?"

She clenched her fingers together and settled them on her hips. Too many words were tumbling around in her brain and she had to fight herself to choose what to say. "You wooed me. You flirted with me all night and I thought you were genuinely taken with me. When you asked me to dance the waltz I agreed, although I did not have permission to dance. After the dance, you laughed at me and left. Everyone at the ball was scandalized, including my mother, who exiled me here."

She caught her breath, the air puffing out like a fog while she struggled to control the anger that boiled up from the memory.

When he didn't say anything, she went on, "You used me as entertainment, and then when you disgraced me, you thought it was funny. You sneered when you deserted me after the dance. It was all a game to you. I was a joke."

He swallowed and nodded. "I understand. I also see that an apology is not enough. I wish I could say you are the only female I used in such a way. I, before Mr. Simmons, I was a different person. I am still not the man he thinks I should be and I don't think I ever will be, but I am changed enough to understand how much hurt I caused you."

Her breath shuddered. She hadn't expected that anything he could say would mean anything to her, but it did. His words now hurt. She had spent so long hating him and his apology cracked open that pain again. All those feelings poured out and she wiped a tear away from her cheek, sniffling.

Slowly, Lord Sudbury said, "I am not poor. And, I do have a name I could offer you."

His words stoppered the emotions pouring from her. "What? Are you proposing what I think you are proposing?"

"I assume having my name would make everything better for you back home."

She shuddered. "I fail to see that I have done anything so horrid as to condemn us to that fate."

He sighed, the relief obvious as he relaxed and skated a little closer. "Thank God. I would make you a poor husband, I am sure. You are very pretty, Miss Moore, but I think you are a bit too energetic to suit me."

She bristled, crossing her arms. "Oh, there are many reasons why you would not suit me either, Lord Sudbury."

He circled around her and nodded. "Let me know if you think of a way for me to properly convey my apologies."

She nodded and he pushed off, gliding back across the lake.

She turned away from all of them and repeated in a high, annoying voice, "'You are very pretty, Miss Moore, but I think you are too energetic.' Well, thank you, sir, you just called me pretty and competent all in the same sentence and I will take both of those."

Lord Sudbury may think he had changed, but he was right when he said he wasn't the man he could be. And then, of all things, to pretend to offer marriage! Of all the things to add insult to injury! Oh, if he truly wanted to apologize, he could go roll around in the muck with the hogs for a while. Why hadn't she asked him to do that?

It felt hollow. The apology, the offer, the man felt unwanted and unworthy. He thought he could skate in a few circles and say a few words and she would forgive him. And, maybe it made her a bad person, but she didn't forgive him. She wasn't sure there was anything he could do to change how she felt about him, and she wasn't sure she completely believed him.

Was there any way he could apologize? There was nothing he could do to change the past.

She looked back at the party across the lake. Katherine clung to Wallace, simpering and probably claiming she needed him for balance.

Emma looked lovely in her white fur and pink coat.

Mr. Simmons wasn't in skates, yet, but his feet held steady on the slippery ice. He had a presence that was hard to ignore, his movements fluid and graceful, but the angles of his body spoke of quiet strength.

From this distance, she could see how he towered over Emma. They made quite the couple. Emma in her beautiful fripperies, like a winter princess, and Mr. Simmons like the hardy knight come to whisk her away to his warm castle.

But they almost kissed last night.

He looked over at her. She felt the shift of his gaze like a shiver up her spine.

A scream tore through the air and Charlotte dragged her eyes away from Mr. Simmons. Katherine's arms flailed about, throwing her off balance on the slick ice. Her arms swung in circles and a skate got caught in her skirt. Her leg went one way, her arms swung another, her body twisted and she was suddenly down in a heap of fabric.

Chapter 8

Just like a true knight, Mr. Simmons quickly scooped up a fallen, bawling Katherine, and carried her off the ice. He set her in the cart the servants had used to bring out their skates and supplies. By the time Charlotte reached them, the entire party surrounded the injured woman, throwing suggestions at her.

Charlotte picked up her skirts and took high steps over the ground, awkward in her skates. She raised her voice to be heard over the ruckus, "Everyone back away! Mrs. Burke will want privacy."

The guests melted away, Aunt Johanna pulling a quiet Wallace with her.

Charlotte quirked a brow at Mr. Simmons. He shrugged and climbed into the cart, pulling Katherine's leg onto his lap. " I will try to keep your leg steady as the cart jostles us back. It's not as if I will become overcome with desire at the sight of a sore ankle."

Katherine's eyes widened and her back straightened, her arms reaching at Mr. Simmons to push him away. "Oh, no, no. You are quite right. I will have to raise my skirt to inspect my ankle." She turned to Charlotte. "I can check it myself. I will just wait here until we are all ready to return."

The widow leaned forward to examine her injury. She winced and yelped, then straightened, a wretched sob tearing from her lips.

Charlotte sighed. "I will check it back at the house. I will be very tender. I promise I have checked my younger siblings for similar injuries."

Katherine pleaded, "But, please, can Mr. Simmons join the rest of the guests?"

He shook his head. "You'll want my help for the ride back."

Katherine bit her lip and nodded. She shrieked when the cart lurched forward and she clung to Mr. Simmons, crying.

Charlotte quickly removed her skates and followed the cart back to the house. She caught up just in time to watch Mr. Simmons, with nary a grunt or breath out of turn, carry Katherine into the house. He set her on a cream-colored settee and then backed away to look out the window.

When he was out of earshot, Katherine whispered, "I beg you not to look. I am sure I am fine and my maid will help me."

"Aunt Johanna will want to know if we need to call the doctor. She would consider herself a poor hostess otherwise."

Charlotte wasn't sure if that was true, but she didn't want to leave a possible injury unchecked. She reached up to undo the fastenings holding up Katherine's wool stockings. Purple and yellow splotches covered Katherine's legs as Charlotte pulled down the material, exposing more skin.

She whispered, "Katherine?"

The woman avoided looking at Charlotte, chewing on her knuckle. "Just check the ankle," she added with a plea, "please."

Charlotte took a deep breath and bunched the stocking up around the middle of Katherine's foot. The ankle was red and already swelling. It was her turn to avoid Katherine's eyes. "Mr. Simmons, I think Katherine should recover in her room. I will not call the doctor," Katherine released a small sigh and Charlotte continued, "but I will prepare something to help ease her discomfort."

Katherine asked, "Willow bark?"

Charlotte nodded. "I think it will help."

She stepped back so Mr. Simmons could carry off the damsel in distress.

HE HAD MEANT TO BE a perfect gentleman but had glanced over anyway, just in time to see the garish bruises down Mrs. Burke's legs.

Those weren't from falling down the stairs. They weren't from riding or accidents or whatever excuse a woman could give. And there were enough varying colors to the bruises that they had not happened all at once. They happened over time.

They kept happening.

But none of them had been fresh from the last couple of days. Here, she appeared safe.

Save for her actual accident on the ice.

A maid held open the door and he laid her on the bed, on top of the covers.

She groaned, settled back against the pillows, and then sighed, her eyes closed.

Suddenly she opened them. "Thank you for carrying me. You may tell Charlotte I am settled."

It was a dismissal.

He crossed his arms over his chest. "How long ago did your husband pass?"

"Two years." She batted her lashes. "Are you interested in taking his place?"

He ignored her question. "After he passed, did you return to your family?"

"No. I still live in the house with my husband's mother and brother."

"Ah. And the brother inherited?"

She paused and slowly blinked, looking away. "Yes."

"Do you not have the option to return to your own family?"

"No. Or I would have done so."

"I see." He bowed his head. "Rest, Mrs. Burke, and get better."

He ignored the inquiring look from the maid and left. Still in his coat, he left the house and returned to the lake. Sudbury had roused everyone's spirits again, showing off his antics and movements on the ice. Henry still hadn't put on skates and if the rosiness of everyone's noses meant anything, the party wasn't long for the activity anyway.

On the way back, he walked next to his friend. "What do you know of Mrs. Burke's family? Do we know the late Mr. Burke's brother?"

"Not really. I've seen him before. He frequents mills and bets heavy. I've heard he boxes but I've never sparred with him."

Henry held a quiet rage down in his throat. "A fighter, is he?"

Sudbury gave him a funny look. "I suppose. I always thought there was an edge to the man I didn't care for. And that's coming from me."

Henry eyed the elder Mrs. Burke, an old friend of his godmother's. A robust woman with drooping eyes and constantly adorned with an ostentatious feather somewhere on her person, she wasn't someone he had spoken with.

She hadn't seemed too worried over her daughter's fall. The elder Mrs. Burke was such a longtime friend of his godmother's that he wasn't sure what to think of the woman.

But her son? A man inclined to fight and whose sister by marriage was found with bruised legs? Henry had quite a few opinions forming of him.

At the house, he found Miss Moore scurrying down the hall, a small jar of something in her hands. She turned when he said her name and stepped into the privacy of the library. He followed, nearly bumping into her when she turned suddenly just in the doorway.

"Obviously you will need to leave the door open. This is not a meeting in a dark, secluded hallway, Mr. Simmons."

His actions last night had been less than gentlemanly and the sharp bristling of her body language clearly indicated her feelings on the matter.

He winced and held up his hands. "It will remain wide open, Miss Moore. Perhaps I should apologize?"

"I want men to stop doing things that necessitate apologies. You would be the second one today."

He didn't care to be another notch on her apology belt. "I am not sure if that means you desire my apology."

She made a breathy, exasperated sound, then glossed past the issue. "Mrs. Burke merely has a sprained ankle. She will miss the decorating tonight but will hopefully come around just in time to travel back home. She said she wanted to make sure she had plenty of time to recuperate and I agreed. I will speak with my aunt and of course Mrs. Burke may stay longer if it is needed."

He murmured, "It will probably be necessary."

"I spoke with Wallace a moment ago. He feels awful. Mrs. Burke has been rather, er, clingy. I am sure he didn't realize she genuinely needed his assistance."

"She has taken quite an interest in Wallace."

Maybe this Christmas party was not only about meeting Miss Lawton. His godmother could have other plans up her sleeve.

Miss Moore wrinkled her nose. "She has. At least now that she is resting, that is one less thing for me to worry about."

He glanced in the hall behind him and took a step into the room, a step closer to Miss Moore. Last night, she had felt untouchable in a way that made him want to break the rules. Now she arched those brows at him and reminded him to stay within the boundaries of etiquette.

Should he share with her that he saw the bruises, too? Did Miss Moore realize what they meant? He asked, "Do you think it would be appropriate for me to check on her again tonight? Perhaps together, we can bring some decorations to her room and she can instruct me on where to hang the greenery."

Miss Moore's face lifted to his, her smile radiating her pleasure. "That is a wonderful idea. What a dear you are, Mr. Simmons."

She may not think him so dear if she knew he was restraining himself from pulling her back into the room with him. And closing the door.

Chapter 9

Charlotte sat next to her aunt while they waited for everyone to join them. It was difficult to admit, but she felt a trifle festive.

She had worked so hard folding the flowers and now all of her work would actually amount to something. The storms from autumn had given way to a cold, bleak winter, and everyone's spirits needed the lift of a beautifully decorated home.

Katherine was still in her room but the elder Mrs. Burke sat in a chair on the other side of Aunt Johanna. The woman tapped her cane on the floor and shifted her lips into a disapproving pout. It was a facial expression Charlotte didn't think she could mimic.

Charlotte stood and and excused herself from the group.

The servants used ladders to put up the greenery in the hall. Everywhere else, the mantels, shelves, and over any doorways, would be up to the guests. It had been Aunt Johanna's idea to pair the groups into teams of two and send them to different rooms to decorate. Each team would be accompanied by a maid or footman and the general idea was to make sure Mr. Simmons was paired with Emma.

Aunt Johanna had noticed how little the two interacted. She wasn't sure why they weren't getting along but she was determined to make it work.

Charlotte thought it more of a matter of pride. Her aunt didn't want to be wrong about her decision to pair the two.

Piles of greenery and spools of string lay on carts or tables. Back in the drawing room, everyone, minus Katherine, gathered. Aunt Johanna listed names and places and sent everyone off on their way. That meant Charlotte was paired with her cousin to do the dining room.

She pointed at the mantel, over the doorway, held up pieces of evergreen and holly, asked him to tie things, hold things, reach things, whatever she needed, Wallace agreed.

He was so boring.

While moving a small bunch of mistletoe over to her satisfaction, he quietly asked, "How is Mrs. Burke?"

Charlotte waved her hand, indicating the mistletoe needed to move a bit more to the right. "She is on the mend. I gave her a tincture and she is resting. It is nothing that can't be fixed in time."

He moved over the mistletoe and attached it to the frame around the doorway. He was tall enough to be a spectacular help. It was rather a shame he was so dull.

He said, "She had asked for help getting out on the ice and I . . ."

Charlotte quickly filled in the silence, "It wasn't your fault."

"But-"

"It was an accident, Wallace. Don't be such a nincompoop."

"A nincompoop. Thank you, Charlotte. Eloquent as ever."

"If you feel so awful, find some flowers or something for her room. I thought you would be grateful to not have her hanging on you anymore."

He stared at her. "That is a good idea. I shall bring her flowers."

Charlotte spun in a slow circle, her eyes roving over each wall to check the balance of greenery. She pointed to an empty corner. "Do you think something could hang over there?"

She bunched up some greenery, threw some holly at it, and arranged it in the vase in the corner like a bouquet. "There."

"It does look nice."

"Thank you. And thank you for helping, Wallace."

"Am I free to go?"

"Yes, I suppose you are. I have to check on everyone else."

She turned in one more slow, assessing circle. In the doorway, Wallace stopped and said, "Charlotte?"

"Yes?"

"I know you are in a hurry to return home, but you have matured admirably since your arrival a few years ago."

Matured? A clawing feeling rippled through her chest and she turned on him, annoyed. "Are you insinuating that I was not mature when I arrived?"

That was preposterous. As the oldest, she had spent so much time caring for her siblings, helping her mother with the housework, potting, planning, and preparing. How could he say, after all that, she hadn't been mature?

Her lips tightened when quiet cousin Wallace stood his ground. He said, "I am saying that while here, you have been able to focus on yourself and who you want to be. You spend your time wishing for something you don't have, but you would be happier if you appreciated the things you already possess. Maybe back at your home you were drowned out a little in your large family. But here, you are handling this entire party remarkably well, and you have balanced your strong personality and your work."

He was wrong. She developed only as Aunt Johanna allowed. "Oh, yes. All these years doing exactly what Aunt Johanna wanted of me have helped me be happy with myself. Go away, Wallace."

He sighed and left. She sat down hard in a dining room chair, fuming. Why was it that others always presumed to know better? Maybe if they opened their eyes a little wider, they would be able to see past their own pompous noses.

She sprung up from the chair and stalked from the room. She didn't have time for this. She didn't have time to be angry or to think about why Wallace was so wrong about things he didn't understand.

She had to check on the guests.

Mr. Lawton and her aunt were instructing a footman in the drawing room. The elder Mrs. Burke commanded Lord Sudbury about in a way that made Charlotte smirk. And in the breakfast parlor, she was surprised the greenery wasn't frosty for all the warmth emanating between Emma and Mr. Simmons. She was equally surprised to notice there was not a maid or footman around, either.

She stepped into the room and crossed her arms over her stomach. "I am done in the dining room. Do you need help?"

Emma smiled. "No. We are done."

The decorations were sparse, there was no mistletoe, little ribbon, and she only counted two folded flowers. "Would you mind if I added a sprig of holly here?"

Emma nodded. "Please do. I really have no eye for this. Is my father still in the drawing room?"

"He should be."

With a sweep of her skirts, she was gone, leaving Charlotte alone with Mr. Simmons.

He held up a stick of evergreen. "I am at your service."

She pointed to a vase. "In the dining room, I made a bouquet."

Mr. Simmons grabbed some more greenery and she watched while he arranged evergreen and hawthorn with a few of her golden flowers and some festive red ribbon. He held out the bouquet and asked, "Like this?"

She laughed, "Mr. Simmons, where have you been all my life? A man with an eye for aesthetic."

He took a step closer and she realized what she had said. His eyes smoldered, conveying a heat that immediately warmed her stomach and made her swallow. His voice was low and soft, a sound that sent shivers down her back, he said, "I am glad you like it."

Was he still talking about the bouquet?

He placed the greenery in the vase and held up a handful of her folded flowers. "After all your hard work, where would you like me to place these?"

With that, the heat was gone and she offered him a small, relieved smile, pointing to each corner over the doorway.

He grabbed another sprig of greenery and held it up in the middle of the wall. "Should this go here?"

She laughed and shook her head while he pretended to attach the piece to the seat of a chair. "Maybe Mrs. Burke won't see it and will sit on it."

"That's a beastly thought!"

They both laughed and he pretended he would stick it under the table. "It will tickle someone's knees and we can wait to see how long it takes them to figure out what it is."

"Mr. Simmons, we can't!"

But she was laughing.

He held it up over her. "How about suspended randomly in the air, right here?"

She looked up at the little sprig with long, skinny leaves. "Mistletoe?"

Chapter 10

He smiled down at her, everything from his shoulders on up filling most of her vision, except for that mistletoe. He said, "I believe this means something."

She should take a step back. She knew she should, for so many reasons, but her feet didn't agree and here she stood with him underneath the mistletoe. She said, "Can you hold it and kiss me at the same time? If it lowers, then it's not technically over us."

He arched a brow at her and cocked his head diagonally. "Are you offering me a challenge?"

"I don't think that's what I meant when I said it."

His arm straightened above them and the other looped around her waist.

She said, "What if someone sees? It will look scandalous."

He dipped his head a little lower, his eyes focused on her mouth. She took in a nervous breath, catching the musk of his soap and something his valet likely brushed on his boots. He smelled so masculine. Then his hand pushed gently on her back and he pulled her closer. He made a point of glancing up at the mistletoe and then back down. His lips hovering over her, he said in a husky voice, "Still there. Are you ready?"

She glanced up, too. There was no way she could let him kiss her. "I don't suppose-"

He brushed his lips over hers, a slow, casual brush, before pulling away. "I'm not sure the mistletoe will be satisfied with that. I think you have to actually kiss me back."

She pursed her lips. "You're making up rules."

His eyes were completely fixed on her mouth. "Keep your lips just like that, and then when you feel like it, relax."

He dipped his head down again and pressed his warm lips against hers. It felt silly to stand there like a statue, and he felt so nice, it couldn't hurt anything to enjoy the moment. She tilted her face a little to the left and softened her mouth, pressing back against him. His arm around her tightened, and she heard his exhale before he tilted his own head and pressed harder against her.

Something warm and a little shocking flicked over her lower lip. She pulled back, sucking in a deep breath. "Was that your tongue?"

He didn't loosen the grip around her waist but he lowered the mistletoe. "Can I stop pretending now and just kiss you?"

No. She couldn't let him take advantage of her.

But the gentle way he held her added to the tingle of expectation skimming down her spine. His hand around her, his chest pressing closer to her, the warmth of him seeping through her dress.

Something this wonderful couldn't be right.

And it wasn't. He wasn't meant for her.

She pulled back, stumbling a bit as her gaze struggled to fix on him. She blinked and screwed her brows together in frustration. "How could you do this?"

"Kiss a pretty woman under the mistletoe?"

She shook her head. "I'm not meant for you."

He crossed his arms and leaned against the table, clearly hauling his pride to front and center. "Says who?"

"My aunt! Your godmother! I know," she put her hand to her forehead, "why you need an heiress like Miss Lawton. Why you need to marry as Aunt Johanna says."

He suddenly straightened, a red flush creeping up his neck. "I lead my own life, Miss Moore. Other people can try to tell me what to do and who to be, but ultimately, I make my own decisions."

Easy for him to say. He had access to his own money, his own land, his own servants, and staff, and banks, and all the things men were able to access that gave them the freedoms she did not have. So easy for him to stand there, prideful, and declare how he would live his own life.

He stepped closer and said, "My decision was to kiss you, not Miss Lawton. So far, the more time I spend with you, the more I like you. The more I look forward to seeing you again. The more I wonder what your lips might feel like against mine." He took another step closer. "I decided I was done wondering. And I don't regret my decision. I enjoyed our kiss and I would do it again if you let me."

His eyes held her pinned to her spot while she floundered for something to say. She felt a little scornful, but something else, a little warmer, a little fuzzier, swayed in the back of her mind. Something that told her she would kiss him again, too.

She waved her hands in the air. "Drat it! Drat you!" She stalked from the room. "Drat all men!"

She slammed the door behind her, wishing she knew stronger expletives.

MISS MOORE IGNORED him when he entered Katherine Burke's room. It was almost dinner and he was to carry Mrs. Burke down to the dining room.

On the one hand, he was flattered at her confidence in his physical prowess. Could he carry Mrs. Burke down the stairs and later to the drawing room? Yes. For Miss Moore, he could.

He felt like he should regret speaking to her so harshly earlier, but he couldn't. It was true he had been asked to come here to see if he would match with Miss Lawton. That didn't mean he had to leg-shackle himself to someone who would make his life miserable. His godmother would have to understand that.

Johanna was haughty, but not unreasonable. And she had loved her own husband deeply.

Something was holding Miss Moore back and based on his experience with women, it was probably her desire to marry a wealthy man. Just because Miss Moore could be pleasant when she wanted to, was very attractive, and somehow called to a sixth sense of his in a way no other woman had, didn't mean she didn't want a fortune.

She was just another woman turning away from him because no matter his manners, or good intentions, he just wasn't rich enough.

Sure, he could haul a female down the stairs, but could he buy her fancy white satin gloves or green shawls?

Across the room, Wallace waited by the fireplace. He had helped Miss Moore hang up the decorations around the room but Henry suspected Wallace had an ulterior motive.

Miss Moore, still staunchly ignoring him, folded the blanket over and stepped aside to let Mrs. Burke's maid slide slippers onto her feet.

Henry scrunched his face in disgust, remembering the widow's bruises. He glanced over at Wallace again. Did he know?

The maid stepped back to hold Mrs. Burke's hands as she slid over. Her skirt bunched up, exposing the wrapping around her ankle and, as she shifted her legs over, the bruises just above it.

Wallace's eyes widened and Henry gave a curt nod at the man to acknowledge that he had seen it, too. Wallace stalked over to the bed, cutting Henry off, and scooped Mrs. Burke up himself. Her maid fluttered around them, tucking the skirt down a few moments too late.

Miss Moore hurried forward. "Wallace, are you sure?"

He snapped, "I've got her."

With that, he strode from the room, Mrs. Burke clutching his shoulders. She didn't seem to mind the change in plans at all.

Miss Moore tangled her fingers in the hair over her forehead, pulling strands free from her evening coiffure. "What was that about?"

"Do you really not know?"

"You don't need to be patronizing, thank you."

He held up his hands in surrender. "It wasn't my intention to sound patronizing. Your cousin Wallace has a *tendre* for Mrs. Burke."

"But it is so out of character for him to..." She trailed off, waving her hand in the direction of the doorway.

"Perhaps you underestimate your cousin."

"She has been so awful to him. I don't understand what he would see in her."

"Their attraction is their business." He paused and added, "But he would be good for her."

She huffed and stalked past him, her arms swinging. He caught her hand and held her back. "Miss Moore, I don't want to apologize, but I don't want you upset with me. I think we can enjoy the rest of Christmas."

"It sounds like you want to have your cake and eat it."

"I have never cared for that expression."

"Because it hits too close to the truth for you? What do you want from me? You don't want to apologize for earlier and yet you want me to act as if I am the good, accommodating female. And if I don't forgive you without an apology, then I am succumbing to my emotions. Is that right?"

"That is not at all what I said. I don't want to apologize because I meant what I said. I am not interested in Miss Lawton and she is clearly not interested in me. I do not feel sorry for kissing you."

Her eyes flicked to his and at that moment, the fading orange light of the sunset burst through the window in just a way that illuminated the soft gold strands of her hair. He sensed a sensual heat in her eyes. His fingers grasped hers even tighter and then he let her go.

She slowly pulled her hand away from his and turned away. "I must follow Wallace. Dinner will be served in a few minutes."

His heart tightened in his chest. She confirmed that she wasn't interested in the likes of him. But then she paused at the doorway. He hadn't realized the amount of tension he had been holding in while he waited for a response from her. She smiled at him, just a small one, and said, "No more mistletoe pranks, please. But, well," she bit her lip, "will you play snapdragon again later?"

He let out his breath and nodded. "I believe so. Would you care to join us?"

Her smile grew and she silently nodded before disappearing around the doorframe.

Chapter 11

"Oh my."

Charlotte watched the servants drag the giant yule log into the drawing room. She glanced at her aunt before rushing forward and insisting they pick it up. "You cannot drag this on the fine carpet."

The footmen looked down at their feet as if they had never seen the floor before. To keep her hand from covering her face in frustration, she ground her teeth and grabbed up a fistful of her wool shawl. She took a deep breath and said, "It looks very heavy but I chose you two for a very good reason."

The footmen glanced between each other. "Yes, ma'am."

They carried the large yule log to the fireplace and set it down.

Aunt Johanna rose from her chair, her gray dress offset by a large ruby necklace that sparkled merrily in the candlelight. "It has been a happy Christmas Eve and we will finish the night around the warmth, luck, and new beginnings that a yule log promises. I have prepared wine that we can pour over the yule log as an offering while we each make a Christmastide wish. Tonight, while the log burns, we can think of it burning away everything that has weighed us down this past year so we can look forward to tomorrow, Christmas, with a light heart."

In a graceful sideways arc, she swung her arm, a matching ruby bracelet sparkling on her wrist. Everyone turned to the tray of wine glasses, one for each of the guests.

The group cheered as one end of the long log caught fire.

Lord Sudbury already had his wine glass in hand. "If I may go first?"

He stood over the fireplace with his eyes closed, his brows tugged together as he thought of his wish. Or, Charlotte thought, more likely he was trying to count all his past transgressions, hoping they really would burn away.

If only it was so easy. It would take a lot more than a pagan tradition for her to forgive him. There was only so much a yule log could do.

Lord Sudbury poured a small drop of wine onto the log. The fire sizzled for a second and Lord Sudbury stepped away, grinning. "Who is next?"

Charlotte clutched her wine glass as she watched Mr. Lawton and then Emma take their turns. After everyone made their wish or cast off their past grievances into the fire, a congratulatory cheer went around the room.

Did everyone have things they wanted to leave in the past?

Wallace helped Katherine over. She had some things to ask for, starting with the quick healing of her ankle and, probably, wishing to snare Wallace in marriage. Was she looking for a new beginning?

Better yet, was Charlotte looking for a new beginning? She took a tiny sip of the claret she would offer to the yule log. She would wish to go home.

That was what she wanted, wasn't it? She wasn't supposed to like being here. It was a punishment.

When Charlotte was with her mother, she tried to be quiet and proper in the background. She knew how to murmur something polite when needed, how to act demure, and she understood what was wanted of the perfect English miss. That was what Mama wanted.

But Charlotte had never quite been able to do it all.

And finally, that fateful night, Charlotte had broken the rules. One rule, really. Or maybe a lot of rules all at once. It was the final straw in a long line of instances of not quite being what her mother wanted her to be and the constant censure had become suffocating. All it had taken was one handsome man to push her over the edge.

A perfect maiden wouldn't have let one rakish smile shatter her shell.

Yet Charlotte had crumbled terribly and completely.

The thing was, those freeing moments of deciding for herself, of choosing to be whisked across the dance floor, still held a certain golden glow. She had chosen wrong, but maybe Mr. Simmons was on to something.

She had been here three years, and maybe she didn't have to feel quite so sorry for her actions. She had enjoyed the waltz. Was there any way she could have waltzed and not been sent away?

If she had danced with someone else, someone who hadn't turned the waltz into a joke, maybe that night would mean something else. If she had danced with a true gentleman, was there a way she could have led the change she wanted?

That night, when she agreed to dance, she envisioned showing everyone that the waltz wasn't the gaudy, depraved dance her mother thought it was. There was a way she could have danced and had things turn out.

If only Mr. Simmons had been there that night.

She snorted at herself. Now she was the one who wanted to have her cake and eat it.

On some level, she had to admit that she knew she shouldn't have agreed to waltz. Yet she had chosen to do it anyway. Some small, rebellious part of her had been tired of the constant toll of expectations. Eat breakfast this way to set an example for the younger ones, practice these lessons, visit these friends and neighbors, discuss only these topics, never discuss those topics, only discuss these topics if you sound like this, sit this way while discussing these topics, serve the tea, play this instrument, wear these clothes...

She hadn't been a person.

Charlotte looked down at her gown of gauze and blue satin, her puffed sleeves just the level she wanted and trimmed in a pretty ribbon she had chosen. Aunt Johanna had let her choose her own dresses before the party. She called it a gift in the giving spirit of Christmastide and for the sake of the party.

Her mother had never let her choose her own dresses and never approved a color beyond white, ivory, or a color so pale and insipid it was lost in the candlelight.

With her aunt, it had been thrilling to sit and look over the fashion prints and fabric and point at designs and colors and for the first time, wear something that felt *right*. Like her clothes could match how she wanted people to see her. Not necessarily as a simpering marriageable miss, but as a woman capable of managing this house party.

Something Mr. Simmons didn't see as a bad thing. Nothing about her clothes or her attitude had turned him away. On the contrary, it was the perfect Miss Emma Lawton he didn't care for.

It was his turn to make a wish over the yule log. He rested a hand against the edge of the fireplace and leaned forward, staring a moment into the fire. Orange licked and flared over the edge of the log, a warm steady glow fed by the group's wishes.

He could be wishing for something practical, like a good harvest, fair growing weather, maybe a new roof. But from the moment he dripped his wine onto the log, she wasn't so sure. Mr. Simmons had faith in his capabilities and he was determined to bring his land up to value. A man like him would wish for something he was less certain about.

He glanced over at her and smiled, saluting her with his wine cup. "Your turn, Miss Moore."

Even Aunt Johanna had made her wish. Charlotte was the last guest standing.

She blinked and walked up to the log. The wood snapped and sizzled and a heady fresh wood scent wafted from the fireplace. There was another snap and a little sparkle of flames as some of the previously burned wood shifted over. It was true this was a pagan tradition, but what if this special piece of wood really could burn away her worries?

She could use a little luck and a wish. Would she go home? She didn't know. Did she still want to go home? She wasn't as sure as she was before. She wanted to go home but on her own terms. She didn't want to go back to that performing act of being a perfect miss.

But knowing what she didn't want didn't help her to decide what she did want. The future stretched ahead of her like an early morning fog over a wide field. She needed the luck of the yule log more than she realized.

The past few years had felt so uncertain. They had been difficult, demanding, and at times a little dreary. But they had also held moments of change. A change that, while confronted with the task of making a momentous wish, she hadn't considered before.

I wish...

She dribbled a little wine over the log. *First, I hope you enjoy that offering as much as the rest of us.*

She giggled.

I wish...

There was too much to consider. She wanted to glance around the room, hesitate, stall. She didn't know what to wish for.

There was only one thing, out of it all that she truly wanted.

I wish to be happy with who I am.

Chapter 12

"Where is everybody?"

Charlotte blinked up at him, her wide eyes scanning the room as if there were people hiding behind the table or in a cupboard.

He said, "They went somewhere else. The kitchen is ours."

He knew he was being vague, but all was fair in love and snapdragon, especially when Sudbury started drinking. The wine for the yule log had been very good, dare he say French imported, wine. Sudbury had not held back.

He didn't need Charlotte around Sudbury's kind of drunken revelry. And, as much as he tolerated his friend, he didn't want him scaring Charlotte away again.

She took small, tentative steps up to the table as if she were scanning it for traps. "Is it just us? Won't you miss spending time with your friends?"

"Honestly, Miss Moore, I would rather spend the time with you. I have been looking forward to this."

He was standing too close to her and knew it. He had thought it over and supposed after what Sudbury had done, Charlotte was guarded around men. He didn't want to make her nervous and was determined that tonight would be about proving himself trustworthy. He didn't have a fortune, but he had loads of honesty.

She said, "I still don't understand how you can be friends with him."

"That's a long story." He opened the bottle of brandy. "My father was a gambling drunkard. When he died and I inherited a crumbling pile of brick and failing farmland, I was shocked. I wasted time telling myself it couldn't be that bad, that there was money hidden somewhere, but there wasn't. I worked very hard to turn myself around to try to fix what my father had ruined."

"One of my solutions was to find an heiress." He scratched the back of his head and gave a hollow laugh. "If marriage is off the table, I seem to have no problem in engaging the attention of a woman. But once I want marriage, she is no longer interested in me. I hated to spend time away from my estate, but I visited London more and more with the intention of finding a wife.

"One night, after a very particular rejection, I decided to walk home and be alone with my thoughts. Then I caught a man climbing out of an upper window. He lied and said the door was locked. Then, the real owner of the house, an angry husband, caught Sudbury and there was an altercation, and Sudbury and I ended up friends. I saw in him a bit of myself before my father passed. A fun part that I had denied was still inside me for fear of what it might lead to.

"Over the last three years, Sudbury and I have balanced each other. Neither of us is the wild young man he used to be. When you live the kind of life Sudbury does, it is hard to feel comfortable with the people around you. I think that is why we stick together. We trust each other."

Miss Moore remained silent. She didn't like Sudbury and Henry couldn't blame her. He pushed the container of raisins to her. "I'll pour the brandy. Would you sprinkle in the raisins?"

She nodded, cupping a handful and pushing one past her lips. Her finger pressed a little against her mouth. If he grabbed a raisin and fed her one, would he get to touch her mouth, too? Trace around her lips, brush his finger against her cheek?

Her eyes flicked to him and she swallowed.

So did he. "I said to sprinkle them in, not to eat them."

"I like raisins."

He smiled at her comment. She had a way of responding that held just a touch of defiance and argument. It was bold in a way he wasn't used to hearing from a lady.

When he had arrived, he thought he didn't care who he married. That one English heiress was as good as the next. There was something about Miss Moore that drew him in, like a sailor to the sea. Every time he entered the waters, he knew there was still a vast ocean waiting for him. There was more and it called to him.

And he was the one snared up in the wild beauty of it all.

The hair that was always a hairpin away from tumbling free, the shimmering gray of her eyes, the way her face lit up with excitement when he set the brandy on fire.

He promised himself he would not try to kiss her tonight. At the time, he thought he had a good reason for that, but watching the reflection of the fire in her eyes, her delighted expression, the set of wonder on her open mouth, he doubted his decision.

After all, she was here with him tonight and she couldn't know how much that meant to him.

He stepped closer to her, explaining, "The fire doesn't burn as hot as one fed by, say, wood. The alcohol burns rather quickly but," he snatched a raisin out, "probably isn't going to cause any serious damage."

She turned to look up at him, her shoulder tucked into the crook of his. He was standing much too close. And she probably tasted like sweet raisins.

She said, "Serious damage? You mean, I could be injured."

"It is fire."

See? He could be a little caustic and sarcastic, too.

Her lips turned up in a devious way as she considered the platter in front of them. She wanted to play in the fire, he could see the desire burning there. She reached her hand up and he followed the trail of her delicate fingers. Suddenly, she curled them into her palms and drew her hand back, her expression hardening.

He heard a shaky intake of breath.

He grabbed another one and held it out to her. "It's okay. Truly. Common sense tells you to hold back, to not do it, that fire is hot and will hurt you. But sometimes, the things that feel the hardest to obtain are the ones most worth getting."

She shook her head at him. "You grabbed the raisin, you should have it. If I eat another raisin, it will be because I've obtained it on my own."

"Is that important to you?"

Her eyes watched his mouth while he popped in the raisin. "It is."

The current fire was dying. He would need to drain it and pour in fresh brandy.

While he did so, she said, "I am not sure what this is."

"Snapdragon."

"Ever so helpful, Mr. Simmons."

"Henry."

"I couldn't call you that."

"Of course you can."

She leaned forward on the table. "Are we just friends today and tomorrow? For the party? When you go home, is our friendship over?"

"Are we friends? If you think so, I will always consider you to be one, no matter the distance."

"But we will realistically never see each other again. You will go home. I am to go home, too, I hope."

A tiny tug in his chest gave him pause. He set the brandy bottle back down, mid-pour. "I cannot marry Miss Lawton. For some reason I do not understand, we don't suit. That leaves me in this odd position where I still find myself considering marriage, yet I am open as to who I marry."

"Don't you need an heiress?"

"An heiress would make my life a lot easier. If I don't marry an heiress, I am condemning a woman to a life she may regret."

"I am not an heiress."

He stepped up to her again and put his hands around her upper arms, looking down at her. "You understand, then, why I can be interested in you, but I would ultimately leave it up to you. You would have to decide. I am here." He brushed back a lock of her hair. "I think you are beautiful. I have enjoyed myself when I am with you. But you have to decide, too."

Her throat seemed to stutter over her words as if they were thick or foreign. "You are letting me decide?"

"Of course. You deserve nothing less."

Her face slowly changed, her lips relaxing into a wide smile, her face tilting up to him, and her eyes resuming their cheery sparkle. "Light the brandy again, Henry."

He stared at her a moment longer, fighting his urge to kiss her. He wanted to tease her lips and feel her murmur his name again. He wanted to kiss down her neck and feel the vibrations of her throat against his lips when she said it again. He wanted to-

He lit the brandy. She yelped when the flames licked across the platter and her hand darted forward to snatch a raisin.

She held it up like a prized trophy. "I did it!"

He grinned back at her. "You did! Miss Moore, I could kiss you!"

She said, "I suppose when we are alone, you may call me Charlotte."

He could mutter her name all over her body. She had no idea what she was doing to him, the things he was imagining.

Her eyes met his over the burning platter. Maybe she had some idea.

He forced his eyes down and issued a challenge. "The one with the most raisins before the fire burns out is the winner."

Chapter 13

Her feet clunked up the backstairs a little heavier footed than she intended.

Did she dare to hope that the most handsome man she had ever met, the one she shouldn't consider for herself, might actually want her?

A shimmering, soft giddiness descended down her body as she realized she wanted to be with him. She wanted to spend more time with him, talk to him, play games with him, even, dare she say, kiss him.

A lot.

All the kisses.

Whatever came after kisses, the warm, velvet sensation that took over whenever she thought of him told her she wanted that, too.

Which meant considering marriage. They could court, go through the motions of an engagement, and he would meet her parents.

Charlotte slid her hands down her cheeks. Her parents would be a hurdle she did not look forward to jumping. If Mama didn't approve, what could Charlotte do about that?

A large part of her knew she couldn't consider Henry if Mama didn't approve, but a small, rebellious voice deep inside of her said maybe there could still be a way.

He seemed determined to have her. And there was that warm, velvety feeling again.

She blinked dry eyes.

At the other end of the hall, muffled footsteps signaled someone coming up the grand stairs. Charlotte quickly dashed for her room but Aunt Johanna came into view too soon.

"Charlotte? What are you doing about?"

She could hear the tired, scratchy sound of her own voice. "Checking a few last things. Tomorrow is Christmas, after all."

Aunt Johanna looked just as tired when she nodded. "I had a few things to check on as well. I've been meaning to speak with you alone."

At some point in her life, Charlotte would get a good night's sleep. It had to happen eventually.

Aunt Johanna shuffled some papers around on the small escritoire in her bedroom. "I have two concerns to discuss with you. The first involves a letter I received from your mother."

Mama? Was her family finally writing to bring her home? This was it!

There was another excruciatingly slow moment in which the only sound was paper shuffling and Aunt Johanna clearing her throat while Charlotte bobbed on her toes. "Ah. Here it is. I am trying to remember the name of the young man." She tapped her finger on the paper. "Your mother wrote to say she has been speaking of you, gauging reactions from her friends and neighbors. She says everyone misses you and when you return, she would like to have a small party."

The bright bubble of jubilation expanding in her chest grew and Charlotte was near to bursting. "I am to go home?"

This was everything she had been waiting to hear. What time was it? Maybe Christmas miracles really did happen.

Aunt Johanna nodded. "Yes, my dear. I am glad you sound so happy since I will surely miss you here."

Charlotte hugged her aunt, holding back the tiny, delighted squealing sounds she wanted to make. "I will miss you, but I miss my family so much right now."

Aunt Johanna deftly patted her on the cheek and extricated herself from the embrace. "Don't go all squeamish on me now. There was one more thing in the letter. A Mr. Fishbottom, Fishburton, Fish-"

"Mr. Fishering?"

"That is probably the name. I understand he is a gentleman of some fortune and he also expressed an interest in your return. Your mother wrote he is in search of a wife."

Charlotte laid her hand over her heart. "In-in me?"

She had grown up doting on Mr. Fishering. He was the handsome, older boy she would think of when she plucked off flower petals. *He loves me, he loves me not, he loves me...*

He was interested in her? Now? Just when she thought she could give everything over for Henry, now the boy she had spent her childhood fantasizing over, the wealthy one near her family, the one her mother approved of, stepped forward?

He had never shown any interest in her before. Was she convenient or did he actually remember her?

In the jumble of her emotions, Charlotte tried to listen to what her aunt was saying.

"That brings me to the other matter. Mr. Simmons."

The feeling drained from her face, leaving behind a sort of numb apprehension.

Always one to forge ahead, Aunt Johanna went on. "You are spending too much time with him. You know why I invited Mr. Simmons and Miss Lawton and your behavior is rather shocking. I was nearly tempted to write to your mother and say you had not quite grasped the intricacies of proper behavior, solely based on your attention to a man I cannot approve of for you. He is in the process of repairing his fortunes, not an easy task, and not a life I would wish for you.

"Miss Lawton, however, has a sizable dowry and is the heiress to everything her father owns. She is not something Mr. Simmons can afford to give up. Charlotte, you know the way these things work. You have your own path set out for you back home and Mr. Simmons has his own path here."

Her aunt may as well have dumped a bucket of freezing water over her head. Charlotte was too tired, her energy drained from the emotional upheaval of the past few minutes, and suddenly she was so lethargic she was near shivering.

She was tired. She was tired of everyone telling her what to do, what was best, who to be, whom to marry, whom to not marry, whom to dance with, whom to talk to, what to say.

She was too tired to think through any kind of rational decision. Right now, her emotions felt as if they had warred with each other, battling through her with everything from jubilation to shame. Her aunt wanted her to submit and it didn't matter what Charlotte wanted. No one ever asked what she wanted out of her life.

She wanted to be happy.

Maybe she would be happier if she submitted. She could go home and be with her family. She had been squealing with delight a few minutes ago.

She shouldn't be so quick to dismiss her original goal. Home would make her happy. She should not cast her life aside simply because one man made her feel like velvet.

Charlotte sagged, her shoulders drooping.

It was enough. Today was enough. Charlotte's feet turned around and she shuffled away. Her hand on the latch, she paused when Aunt Johanna asked, "Don't you have anything to say to me?"

No. Not anymore. Not tonight.

"Charlotte? We're not done."

She was beyond done. Everyone else wanted to tell her how to live her life and no one ever asked what she wanted. "I want to go to bed. I am tired."

She would pay for that comment later.

"That is not the answer I am looking for."

Of course it wasn't. Charlotte was supposed to do exactly what Aunt Johanna wanted at every moment or hell might open up and swallow her. She had spent three years trying to live up to every one of Aunt Johanna's rules and whims. But after following one soul-crushing rule after another, what did Charlotte herself have to show for it?

She crushed all of her feelings and thoughts down into a tiny little ball and swallowed, mentally shoving everything away into a tiny little space inside of her where she didn't have to worry about it.

Tomorrow. Everything would have to wait until tomorrow when she wasn't so exhausted. "Good night, Aunt Johanna. I am, honestly, too tired."

Her aunt gasped, but if she said anything else, it was cut off when Charlotte closed the door.

As she flopped into her own bed, she didn't care what anyone else wanted from her.

Maybe that was why Henry appealed to her. He didn't impose his expectations upon her. He trusted her reasoning and encouraged her to act accordingly. It was shocking how comforting something so simple could feel. And it was unexpected how happy it made her.

She should have felt guilty for walking away or for leaving before given permission. No matter how hard she tried to tell herself that returning home would make her happy, all she could think about was Henry's smile when he won at snapdragon.

Chapter 14

He knew he was grinning on a level that bordered on stupid and it had nothing to do with it being Christmas Day. He couldn't stop thinking about last night. Besides that they had broken quite a few rules by being alone together, he had kept his distance and remained proper.

No hidden mistletoe, no forward advances, no kisses in the dark.

Proper.

The night had been perfect. He enjoyed himself, Charlotte looked as if she enjoyed herself, and they eventually ditched the game to sit on the table, swinging their legs, talking about anything and everything.

He shared his plans for his land and described his house and how it used to look when his mother was alive. She shared how much she missed her own family. She spoke of a younger sister who helped her steal the boys' clothes while they were swimming, let frogs loose before mass, and helped her sew all the ripped hems from running and climbing.

Charlotte wasn't someone who liked to sit still. When he first arrived, there was a sandpaper quality to her manners that he now understood. She was stifled living with his godmother and had nowhere to let out her energy.

He could think of lots of ways to help.

He assumed, with all those extra sisters she had spoken of, that her dowry was small. His aunt wouldn't consider her suitable for him, but he resented that she underestimated him.

From the way Charlotte spoke about her life back home and the little things she wanted now, she would be perfect running Blenworth House. He needed someone capable, someone with the fortitude to help him see the estate repaired.

Someone with an energy to match his own.

He didn't need Miss Lawton. He needed Charlotte.

Her dress was a little more daring today, a low-cut, ice blue dress with lace trim. He watched her waist when she stood to join a new group.

He followed. "I hear there are to be some games this afternoon."

Sudbury and Miss Lawton also turned their attention to Charlotte. She said, "I have pictures that have been cut to be pulled apart and reassembled. The pieces are small enough that I assume this will be no easy task." She turned to survey a table. "Although it looks like Mrs. Burke has already claimed that activity. There are also cards, but we want our activities to reflect the sanctity of Christmas. In a short while, Mr. Lawton has something he would like to read to us, but the afternoon is open for whatever activities suit my aunt's guests."

She turned abruptly to Miss Lawton. "You are exemplary at the pianoforte. I am sure Mr. Simmons would turn the pages for you if you would be so kind as to play us something."

Was he being volunteered to do something with Miss Lawton?

By Charlotte? Did he do something last night to offend her?

A prickle on the back of his neck made him wary. He glanced around to find his godmother eyeing them, her lips pinched, tapping her fan.

He gestured at Sudbury. "I think I have been remiss in the amount of attention I have given my godmother. If Sudbury could step in for me, I will offer to take Mrs. Brancaster about the room."

Sudbury smiled, guided Miss Lawton to the pianoforte, and Henry turned on his heel to head for his meddling god-mother.

She was stern, but she was the only mother figure he had. This thought hit him just in time for him to soften his grimace upon approach. "I have not spent enough time with you this visit." He held out his hand to her to help her stand from the chair. "Would you take a turn about the room with me?"

She flicked her gaze over to Miss Lawton, who had just started the gentle notes of a song. Standing without his offered help, she tucked her hand into his elbow. "This is a nice gift from my favorite godson."

"Only godson."

"Thankfully. One of you is enough. Children never do as they are told."

He reached his free hand over to squeeze her fingers. "Alas, I am no longer a child. Just a troublesome adult, apparently."

She sighed. "Is it so awful that I want a good life for you?"

He countered, "There is more to life than quickly gaining money by marrying someone who doesn't seem to care for me."

She made a gravelly sound of disagreement.

He stopped them in front of the far window, a place as private as they could manage in a crowded room. In a low voice, he said, "You didn't raise me to be stupid."

She startled, as much as the staunch woman could startle, her eyes searching his. "Of course not."

"At some point, you must admit that I am capable of making my own decisions."

Softly, she said, "You don't care for Miss Lawton?"

"I don't think she cares for me. The women get a say in this, too."

She stiffened, her shoulders squaring defensively. "What wouldn't she like about you?"

He chuckled. "Blinded a little, my dear godmother?"

She smiled up at him, her laugh lines creasing on her delicate skin. "Maybe she has an interest in someone else. Her father hasn't indicated anyone or we wouldn't have considered this. He wants to see his daughter married to someone trustworthy."

They watched while Sudbury turned a sheet of music.

His godmother turned away first to look out the window. "I cannot approve of you courting Miss Moore. Her dowry is small and she has someone back home."

Did she? She hadn't given any indication. He got the opposite impression, that she was lonely and wasn't sure what she wanted from her life. That not knowing such a thing bothered her greatly.

Mrs. Brancaster went on, "If Miss Lawton does not suit, I cannot force such a thing. But the flirtation with my niece must stop."

His voice held a hard edge, his pride coming up like a shield. "How far are you willing to go to stop me if I do choose Miss Moore?"

Was she threatening him? Would she change her will, grant her fortune to someone else?

Her eyes shifted over to survey the room. "I will have to think on that. I don't like what you are implying. Excuse me, I see I am needed somewhere else."

She wanted to deter him and was willing to use manipulation to do so.

He watched while Charlotte placed a piece of the cut picture into place. She grinned and clapped, her dazzling delight drawing the attention of the room. Charlotte did that. She had an engaging light inside of her that drew others. Her energy always reflected back in a way that made him want to stand near her brilliance, soaking it into his skin, through to his soul.

But he also had tenants, servants, and people who counted on him.

Just how much was a chance at love worth?

Chapter 15

She had saved this dress for tonight. Her aunt's maid helped pin her defiant hair into something not just respectable, but actually pretty. A few tendrils curled down her face, but these were there on purpose instead of just rebelliously springing free from her coif.

Her dress, a cool green satin with puffed sleeves at her shoulders and gold ribbon around her waist, felt like Christmas. Not the holiday she had been dreading all week. It felt like the joy and warmth of spirit she remembered from when she was a girl.

The maid handed Charlotte a small, wrapped package, about the size of a small book. "This is for you."

It was almost time for Christmas dinner but Charlotte turned the package around in her hands. "For me? From whom?"

The maid grinned. "I promised not to tell."

Charlotte tugged on the string and unwrapped the gift. She hadn't expected anything like this and-

"Oh." She stifled a sob and pulled out a pair of soft, white evening gloves. The same pair she had been looking at in the shop. The maid quietly left Charlotte alone to finish her ensemble. Pulling on her new satin gloves, she couldn't help but think of Henry. Mr. Simmons. She should call him Mr. Simmons now that she had decided to avoid him.

He had known she wanted these.

His thoughtfulness sent a little thrill up her spine. Would he like her dress?

Charlotte smoothed her gloves up her arms and left her room. It didn't matter if he liked her dress. But he should. She felt lovely.

She sighed. It was difficult pretending not to have feelings for someone she definitely had feelings for. And now she had to find a way to thank him.

Emma giggled behind her in the hall. "Will dinner be so dreary? Why the long sigh?"

Charlotte paused for Emma, who was dressed in a creation of white and evergreen. "This small Christmas party has been nothing like I expected. I'm a little shocked that it's nearly over."

Emma lifted her hem a little with her left hand to take the steps. "I have had a wonderful time, though. And I know we are at your aunt's house, but you are clearly the mastermind behind everything. I have truly enjoyed myself and have you to thank."

Charlotte couldn't help but ask, "Oh? Not Lord Sudbury?"

Emma blushed. "I had heard of him before this party. He has been in the gossip papers and for very deserved reasons. But here, he has been a perfect gentleman."

Charlotte turned that information over in her head and couldn't decide how she felt about it. A little resentful? Suspicious?

Emma stopped at the bottom of the stairs, glancing around at the empty hall. "He mentioned he had met you before and indicated it was not under the best of circumstances. He has brought it up more than once and I think it bothers him."

Charlotte quickly cut off that line of conversation. "He apologized and I am trying to leave it in the past."

Emma blinked her blue eyes.

Charlotte continued, "In the past, he did not conduct himself with the best of intentions and I blamed him for the consequences. But I am starting to see that some blame must be put on myself. I, perhaps, have not always behaved with the best of intentions, either."

"You? Oh, but you're so suave and engaging. I have been trying to emulate your energy these past few days."

Charlotte felt a warm blush creep into her cheeks. "My goodness, why?"

"You handle so much and you do it so well. You organized the party, kept us entertained, handled things in the background, and then turned around and smiled at us all. I admire your energy and it makes me doubt my own abilities." She stopped to laugh at herself. "I think I am much too sheltered and spoiled by my father."

Charlotte felt as if she must now return the compliment. "When I first saw you, I thought you were the perfect English rose. You are talented in ways that I didn't have the patience to study and I have been envious of your abilities to behave as the perfect lady."

Emma hooked her arm through Charlotte's. "Now that we are in each other's confidence, will you tell me all the juicy gossip about you and Mr. Simmons?"

Charlotte's warm glow from a moment ago eased back and she sighed again. "There is no me and Mr. Simmons so there is nothing to tell."

"Don't lie to me. I have seen you two together. I think he is perfect for you. I think he is intimidating, a little too serious, and he makes me feel as if he is judging me like I am a horse before a race. But when he's with you, I don't see any of that. You two get along splendidly and make a rather handsome couple, I will add."

Charlotte should at least try to stay the course. "I thought when he stood next to you, you looked like a princess and he the dashing knight. Are you sure you don't care for him?"

Emma groaned. "Not you too. I am sure that I don't care for him."

They were at the drawing room doors and someone was coming down the stairs.

Emma smiled and changed topics. "Ready for dinner? I have been looking forward to this all day. Will there be Christmas pie?"

There was Christmas pie and there was more than one placed around the table so everyone could get a scoop of the slightly sweet, yet mouthwatering and savory meat pie. Charlotte had planned a remove of white soup and other first course dishes littered the table, the nearest to her being the cod and a bowl of sweetbread.

She hadn't meant to be seated next to Mr. Simmons.

Everyone was in good cheer. As usual, as the highest ranking gentleman, Lord Sudbury had escorted her aunt into the dining room. But behind them, no one cared who linked arms.

She wasn't seated next to Mr. Simmons because he chose her. No, not at all. No, he chose to offer his arm to Emma. For a moment, the heiress looked as if she wouldn't take it, but then her perfect manners took over and she demurely left the drawing room on Henry's arm.

Wallace had scooped up Katherine, Mr. Lawton left with the elder Mrs. Burke, and there was Charlotte, as usual, left to enter the dining room all by herself. When her aunt had counted for "even numbers," they had been ruined when Mr. Burke hadn't accompanied the rest of his family.

Charlotte was trying not to let her feelings ruin the steaming, tender slice of roast beef being placed on her plate, but the emotions roiling within her made it difficult. Mr. Simmons gave an inordinate amount of attention to Emma, Wallace was completely absorbed in Katherine, and here was Charlotte, left to stab at her meat.

Her fork clinked against her plate a little too loud and Mr. Simmons glanced over at her.

Cool politeness, he said, "Miss Moore, this dinner is splendid."

That was it? That was all he had to say to her? She shouldn't be upset. After all, she had tried to pawn him off on Emma earlier. Now that he was taking the hint, she shouldn't be mad.

But she was. If she could stab her plate any harder, it might crack, rather like the fragile sense of decorum holding her together.

She had wanted time to sort out her feelings and she had taken all day to determine nothing. She didn't know what to do and her own indecision felt just as frustrating as the rules normally imposed on her. She was struggling to make any decision and it made her feel as if everything would be easier if she gave in and listened to what everyone else wanted.

She must not have been controlling her feelings as well as she thought because Henry's voice softened and he pivoted his shoulders to face her better. "The glazed carrots are delicious. Would you like me to reach the bowl for you?"

She loved glazed carrots. "No, thank you."

He lowered his voice. "I am worried you are upset with me."

She shoved a bite of meat into her mouth and spoke with her mouth full. "What would give you that idea?"

One side of his mouth lifted. "It is nice to meet a woman who enjoys a good bite of meat. Don't let our conversation stop you."

He spooned another helping of carrots onto his plate. "Are you sure you don't want any?"

He knew. She had told him she loved glazed carrots and that they would be on the menu. She spooned a small helping of macaroni onto her plate. "As you can see, I can take care of myself."

His low laugh spiraled down her spine, the sound rich and handsome. "Will there be Christmas pudding? With raisins, I presume?"

Raisins. The newest bane of her existence. She would never eat them again and feel the same. And it was all his fault. Why was he suddenly teasing her after making such a show of choosing his precious heiress?

She turned her attention to Wallace. "Cousin, did you finish the cut picture earlier? I am sorry I could not sit and stay until the end."

He had to finish chewing a bite of potatoes. "We finished and the landscape painting was lovely. I promised Mrs. Burke," he glanced at Katherine, "that I would show her the spot on the property this spring."

Charlotte said, "That sounds like something lovely to look forward to. Something must get us all through the cold days ahead."

She glanced over at Mr. Simmons. Cold, cold days, indeed.

Wallace quickly turned his attention back to Katherine and Henry leaned down to whisper in her ear, "Perhaps there is a way I can warm your thoughts."

Charlotte dropped her fork.

Glancing around to make sure no one else was paying them any attention she hissed back, "What game is this?"

"Game?"

She wanted to smack him. There, right on his wide, chiseled cheek. Drat him.

He said, "You made it clear this morning that you wanted nothing to do with me. I am not sure what I did to offend you."

"You did nothing to offend me."

She pulled her lips in, hiding them, wishing she could take back what she had said. It was true. He had done nothing wrong. It was everyone else telling her they were not meant to be.

In his softest tones yet, he leaned over to whisper, "Did you not believe me when I said I chose you? Knowing what everyone else wants, I choose you?"

Choose?

She wished she had his confidence. She had spent her life trying to live up to everyone else's standards. She wanted, so desperately, to earn their favor. To be the perfect lady they all wanted. Choosing Henry was like throwing all of her hard work away. She would lose all the approval she had spent years trying to gain.

In a smooth motion, he picked her fork up from her lap and held it up to her. She felt her face heat and snatched it back.

He asked, "Will you meet me again tonight?"

"If we are found, I truly will be ruined."

"Not if I married you."

"Are you hatching a plan or proposing in a dastardly way?"

He slowly pulled his fork out of his mouth, chewing a bite of carrots. Then he smiled at her and scooped a spoonful of them onto her plate. "I am not sure. But I can't help that every conversation with you, no matter how spirited, makes me smile. You can't blame me for looking forward to our next meeting."

There was that velvety feeling again, like brushing her fingertips against soft rose petals, except the sensation slid down her whole body.

"I think you might be a rogue, Mr. Simmons."

He winked at her. "Same place and time, Miss Moore. I am counting the hours."

Her carrots tasted better than she remembered.

A footman wheeled in the Christmas pudding and it was quite the show to watch the pudding be scooped and served in equal amounts. Once everyone had a helping, Aunt Johanna gave a small Christmas toast.

"And I'd like to finish by saying that, no matter who gets the lucky coin, I wish all of us luck in health and happiness."

A goodhearted cheer rippled around the table and everyone sipped their wine.

Charlotte watched while Wallace pushed his spoon into the middle of his pudding. He glanced at her and muttered, "No coin here."

Across the table, Katherine's shoulders fell a little when she did the same thing. Charlotte heard her say, "I don't need a lucky coin."

Was it her imagination or did Katherine and Wallace exchange a heated glance?

Feeling as if she had interrupted a private moment, she focused on her own dessert. It was moist and sweet, there were raisins and a hint of brandy and nutmeg. The spice swirled on her tongue and for a moment, the room was quiet as everyone took their first bites of the delicious treat.

Her spoon hit against something hard. She scooped her bite away, telling herself it was probably a nut, but it was difficult to suppress her hope.

There, surrounded by Christmas pudding, was the silver coin. She grinned and looked up to share her good fortune.

She glanced at Henry and something told her she would need all the luck she could get if she wanted to follow her heart.

Chapter 16

The entertainment for the evening had started out related to Christmas but quickly devolved into something else entirely. The original idea had been to play a form of shades, but instead of tracing the shadow of something Christmas themed, they were representing a classical god or goddess.

Without missing a beat, Henry watched as Charlotte smiled at the guests, nodded in agreement, then quickly coordinated with the servants to bring specific items. The more he watched her, the more he wondered whether she understood all the things she accomplished, all while trying to keep everyone else happy.

He hadn't chosen a classical figure yet, mainly because he had thought to do Apollo but Sudbury had beat him to it. Now he stood to the side, racking his brain for a runner-up.

Charlotte sat for her tracing now, holding a cup and a figurine of an eagle to represent Hebe. The perfectly curled tendrils framed her face and it showed in her shadow, giving her tracing an authentic classical look.

He had started the holiday with the assumption that marrying one woman was just as good as the next, but now that he had met Charlotte, he understood how wrong he had been. There were other women and then there was Charlotte.

And he would have her.

Sudbury held the lyre he had chosen to represent Apollo. He had asked for a bow or arrows but had been denied by a frowning hostess.

Even when she put Sudbury in his place she was beautiful.

Henry asked, "Can you play that?"

Sudbury held up the stringed instrument and grimaced. "No, even though it is attributed to Apollo, it feels rather feminine. I wouldn't be caught dead playing it." He then lifted it and strummed, winking. "Do I look beautiful while I play?"

Henry laughed at his friend's kissing face and motioned for him to put down the instrument.

Sudbury asked, "Have you picked your figure, yet?"

"I was thinking Heracles."

"I suppose you could do him. You won't need a prop. Just take your shirt off and flex as if ready to battle a lion." He jutted his chin in Charlotte's direction. "I promise the ladies won't stop you."

They were standing at the back of the room so no one saw when he punched Sudbury in the shoulder.

His friend rubbed at the spot. "I don't think I deserved that."

"I think you tend to underestimate the consequences your actions deserve."

"I can't argue that as you're probably right."

Sudbury was far too jovial this evening. "What has you in such joyful spirits?"

"The holiday, of course."

"No. Really. Why are you in such good cheer?"

"Do you hear yourself? Joy? Cheer? It's Christmas."

"And? What else is it?"

Sudbury gave one of his grins that usually had ladies swooning at his feet. "It is Christmas. I have had good food, lots of wine, and I am happy that this wholesome entertainment is actually fun."

"Fine. Don't tell me what has you so happy,"

Sudbury sighed. "It is my birthday."

"Today? Christmas? Your birthday is on Christmas?"

"Aye. Today I have amassed thirty years."

Henry clapped his friend on the back. "We should have another toast!"

Upon hearing the word "toast," Mr. Lawton turned and raised his quizzing glass at them. At the same time, the butler entered and whispered something to Wallace and Mrs. Burke. Henry said, "I am glad you appear to be enjoying your birthday."

Sudbury grinned again. "I am. Would you like to know why? At this point, I have decided I am tired of caring about what everyone else wants of me. Ten years ago I would have been bored to tears at a party such as this. But now, and this is partially your fault, I don't mind this. I don't feel as if I need to like or dislike certain things so that I appear a certain way. I feel like I am settling into myself."

"You have developed feelings for Miss Lawton."

"I have not."

"You have and you think you need to change for a woman. I thought I would never see the day."

"You are far off the mark, my friend."

Henry snorted.

Sudbury lifted his lyre. "It probably was wise of Miss Moore to not allow me weapons."

"Tomorrow we will return to Blenworth House for a rousing round of fencing. I intend to soundly beat all this wholesome nonsense out of you."

Sudbury saluted. "I accept your challenge."

Henry laughed. "Just a game, not a duel."

The men waited a moment, watching while Wallace stood and quietly left. Mrs. Burke stared at the closed door as if a ghost would walk through it.

Sudbury sighed. "I shall sit with her so you can continue to ogle the lovely Hebe."

"I'm not-"

But his friend was already walking away. And his statement would have been a lie anyway. Miss Lawton was nearly done with her tracing. Charlotte caught Henry's gaze and smiled back, but then straightened when Miss Lawton hissed at her to sit still.

He needed to ask what she would do with the tracings after tonight. He would keep the one of her.

There was a shout from the hallway. Mrs. Burke jumped up and pulled her green shawl around her tighter, her fingers twisting in the cashmere. Sudbury switched his seat so he was between her and the door.

Something was happening out in the hall and Henry wasn't sure what it was, but he shuffled closer to the door, trying to look casual behind Sudbury.

Charlotte looked over to him, her eyes holding her question.

He shook his head. He didn't know what was going on and he didn't want her to worry, yet.

He wasn't the only one who heard the crash, others were glancing at the door, too. He said, much too loud, "Miss Moore, your tracing is almost done and it is lovely."

That redirected everyone's attention except Mrs. Burke's.

The commotion in the hall continued and someone yelled that he would not leave.

The elder Mrs. Burke stood up from her discussion with his godmother. "Is that my son?"

The door burst open, two footmen and Wallace trailing a tall, dark man in a long, black coat. He glowered at his audience, his thin face petulant and severe. "I cannot believe the disrespect I am being shown. On Christmas, no less!"

Everyone stood, facing the newcomer.

Sudbury stood in front of Mrs. Burke and Henry clenched his fingers into a fist.

Wallace, his normally quiet voice now hard, said "You are not welcome here, no matter the day."

Sudbury stepped forward, pretending to brush a piece of lint from his shoulder. "It appears you have not received an invitation to the party and it is rude to burst in on someone else's Christmas."

The man pointed at the elder Mrs. Burke. "How could my mother be invited and not me?" He calmed and continued, "I am sure it is a misunderstanding."

Wallace said, "Even if you had at one point received an invitation, as the master of this house, I revoke it. You. Must. Leave."

Henry presumed the man was Mr. Burke, the brother who inherited the Burke fortune.

Mr. Burke calmly brushed melting snow off his jacket. "If I am to leave, I will take my womenfolk with me."

The elder Mrs. Burke trilled a laugh. "Surely this is all a mistake. My son is welcome to stay the night for Christmas."

Henry wondered if Katherine Burke even realized she was clutching Sudbury's sleeve. Sudbury's valet would be in tears over the wrinkles she caused.

His godmother joined the throng of those with an opinion. "Of course he may stay. We won't want to ruin a perfect Christmas evening."

Wallace's voice rang through the room like a death toll. "No."

Henry's head swiveled between his godmother and Wallace.

She said, "Wallace."

"No."

"You are being unreasonable. We will discuss this in the library."

"No."

"Wallace!"

Wallace signaled the footmen. "I am not discussing this further."

He was the first to grab at Mr. Burke's shoulder. The man thrashed his slender frame, pivoting away. "I will not be manhandled!"

Wallace's face reddened and a vein popped on his neck. He pulled his arm back and launched it at Mr. Burke. The other man was quick-footed and sidestepped the punch.

Mr. Burke yelled, "You would molest me!"

Katherine Burke sobbed, her forehead resting against Sudbury's back, her shawl pulled up to her cheek.

Mr. Burke was a raging hypocrite.

Wallace turned and pulled his arm back again for another go, but women were shrieking and Henry had had enough.

He stepped forward, speared Wallace with a harsh look, and twisted Mr. Burke's arm behind him, locking the man in a tight hold. "I believe you were leaving."

The man sputtered. "Satisfaction. I demand satisfaction for this dishonor."

Henry tightened his grip and propelled the man forward to the open door. Outside, snow swirled in a winter wind. "You are angry and perhaps need to cool your head."

Mr. Burke stumbled, trying to slow their progress by dragging his feet. It didn't matter. The skinny man wasn't a match for Henry's own trained muscles.

"You wouldn't dare toss me out! I am a gentleman!"

"You are an entitled-"

"I challenge you! Dawn! Choose your weapon."

"Pistols, but you don't appear to have a second, so you are wasting your time."

Henry shoved the man outside.

"I will worry about my second. You have nothing to worry about except your imminent demise tomorrow morning."

Henry shut the door in the cur's face.

Chapter 17

Something happened out in the hallway that the men were not talking about with the rest of the party. Aunt Johanna was beyond upset, having swept up to her room in chilly silence, ridding herself of all the disturbing behavior happening beneath her.

The elder Mrs. Burke screeched worse than a fabled banshee and Mr. Lawton used that exact phrase to complain about the noise. Wallace paled and bid Mrs. Burke to retire to her room.

Forced. It was more that he forced the woman to retire.

Charlotte didn't know quiet cousin Wallace could be so commanding.

Emma and Katherine didn't want to retire, so the men left for Wallace's smoking room.

The three youngest women were alone with their worries and Charlotte was tired of twisting her pretty gold ribbon into ruined knots. She stood and smoothed her skirt. "Well, I cannot just sit here any longer."

Katherine dropped her hand from the side of her face and said in a dull tone, "Didn't you hear when Lord Sudbury was asked to be a second?"

Emma gasped and touched her fingers over her heart. "Whose second?"

Katherine put her hand back up to her forehead, which muffled her voice. "It's all my fault."

Emma exchanged a quiet look with Charlotte. How could this be Katherine's fault?

Charlotte sat down on the settee. "I am sure that is not the case."

Katherine sniffled, then sobbed. Emma began to search for a handkerchief and Charlotte patted the widow's thigh.

Katherine blubbered, "Wallace knows that Mr. Burke is, is not," she sniffled, "is not kind to me. That is why he refused to let him stay."

Emma handed over a pretty square of white cotton. Katherine's nose sounded like a musical horn when she blew into it, except for the sound of all the wet snot.

Charlotte said, "It is Wallace's home and he has every right to deny entry to anyone he wishes. I am not sure why exercising his rights should end in a duel."

Katherine sobbed some more. "The way Mr. Burke sees it, Wallace has denied him his right to his property."

There was another high-pitched wail followed by more shaky breaths and sobs. Another loud, wet blow into the cotton.

Charlotte patted Katherine's shoulder. It somehow felt like the thing to do. "Er, would you like some tea? A blanket? Another handkerchief?"

"Y-you are too kind. N-no one has been this nice to m-me in a long time."

No one?

Emma said, "That doesn't make sense. Mr. Burke has not been here. He has no property in this house."

Katherine gasped for breath.

Charlotte cleared her throat but there was no way to say the words in her head without forcing them past the taste of disgust coating her mouth. "Katherine means herself. Mr. Burke considers her to be his property."

Emma exclaimed, "That is nonsense!"

Charlotte wrapped her arms around Katherine's shoulders.

Katherine blew her nose again. In a dark voice, she said, "I am a woman with no rights, no money, and few options."

Charlotte asked, "Is he the reason you have those bruises?"

Emma startled. "Bruises?"

Suddenly Katherine gripped Charlotte's hand. "I can't go back. Life reaches a point where you have to decide to make your own rules and do what feels right."

Charlotte's heart caught in her throat. She had been waiting for someone to tell her that her whole life. And now that someone had, the words twisted in her stomach, making her feel sick.

She never wanted to hear those words under these circumstances.

Charlotte blinked down at her hand, still held in Katherine's. "Are you in love with Wallace?"

For the first time since the men left the room, Katherine gave a tiny, genuine smile. "It has only been a few days. At first, I was desperate to interest any man who would treat me better, but Wallace, he has layers."

Emma chortled. "Layers?"

Katherine nodded and continued, "At first he appears to be a quiet country gentleman. But then we landed on the topic of animal husbandry, and then his love of animals, and something changed between us. Our interactions felt deeper and better connected as we discovered each other's layers. I have been confined to one spot and he has been keeping me company."

That was similar to her interactions with Henry. At first, he looked like a perfect, too-handsome gentleman and she had been wary of him. But the more they talked, the more real he became and the more their discussions touched on things that resonated inside of her.

Her entire life, she had been told she wasn't good enough at being a lady. Now, after three years in exile, her mother wanted her to go back home, show off her perfect manners, and then marry Mr. Fishering like a good daughter.

That was where the rules would take her. Marriage to a man that would continue to push the same constraints on her that she so desperately wanted to shed.

Constraints that Henry would never place on her. She hadn't known him for long, but she trusted that much.

Emma said, "Who asked Lord Sudbury to be a second?"

Charlotte almost forgot how their discussion started.

Katherine blew her nose again and answered behind the cloth. "Mr. Simmons."

Charlotte exclaimed, "Henry!"

Both women raised their brows at her. In the quiet moment, they heard the sound of hooves on gravel and then a commotion at the door. Some feet traipsed back and forth in the hall and then all was quiet again.

Katherine murmured, "That is probably Mr. Burke's second arriving for negotiations."

Emma asked, "For what?"

"The seconds will try to negotiate alternative solutions so the duel itself does not happen. They are illegal, after all."

Emma waved her hand in the air as she stumbled through her response. "Then of course they will come to another solution. It would be ridiculous to, you know, face each other to, you know..."

Charlotte asked, "Why aren't you with them? Doesn't this concern you?"

Katherine said, "The men wouldn't concern a woman in a matter like this. This is about their honor."

Charlotte stood up, her hand clutching her skirt. "No, this is about keeping you safe from that awful man. Hang their honor. Mr. Burke has none. Therefore there can't be anything to negotiate."

Katherine said. "Mr. Burke will not see it that way. And he is dealing with other men whereas he just sees me as-"

She cut herself off to sob into the handkerchief.

Did the men even know how their careless behavior was affecting Katherine? She couldn't sit here or hide in her bedroom, waiting to hear what a gaggle of honor-bound ingrates was planning. Henry wouldn't be so daft, would he?

Charlotte took a deep breath, smoothed her skirts where she had been wrinkling the fabric, and made up her mind. "Well, if all the action is happening in the smoking room, then I suppose that is where I need to be."

Break the rules. Do what feels right.

This time, she had the right man to support her decision.

She swept from the room and neither Katherine nor Emma tried to stop her.

Chapter 18

After the stress of the last hour, Henry's skin felt taut and tired and his thoughts were fraying at the ends as he struggled to concentrate. He was an idiot.

He had land to manage. Tenants who needed him. And on a whim, in a moment of anger and pride, he had thrown all of his responsibility to the wind.

There were so many ways a duel could go, but Henry only saw one path. Burke would not back down; he would not delope. The only path open was to shoot Burke at dawn and face the consequences. At the worst, he would face murder charges and have to leave all of his hard work behind.

Maybe he could manage one of Sudbury's foreign properties.

He thumped into a chair and tried to listen while Sudbury conversed with the man Burke had sent to be his second.

Sudbury crossed his arms and took a step back. "If she doesn't want to return home, none of us will force her against her will. She has sustained an injury and is in the process of healing. If anything, Mrs. Burke," he stressed the title indicating her status as a widow, "will need to stay here until she is fit to travel."

The second, he had introduced himself as Mr. Thornton, flicked at a speck on his arm. "That is not acceptable. There is nothing to negotiate if that one item cannot be met."

Wallace backed away as Sudbury's face turned calm and icy, his mouth twisting into a wicked smile. "You must be unfamiliar with Mr. Simmons. If you had heard of him, you would know that to enter a duel with him is to do Mr. Burke guaranteed bodily harm."

Henry flinched. His friend made it sound like he was promising the results of a facial cream.

Entering a duel with Henry had a guaranteed end result. Pass your pennies over now before the peddler leaves town.

If Thornton had hackles, they would be raised. As it was, the man's thick sideburns twitched when he grimaced. "Mr. Burke is an accomplished shot and is not intimidated by blustering."

Sudbury laughed, a quick, sarcastic sound. "If only I was blustering." He uncrossed his arms and took a step forward, an evil glint in his eye caught by the flicker of the candle. "I can say this. If everything is called off now and Mr. Burke returns home, we will all forget this ever happened. You have our word that none of us will speak of this matter to anyone."

Thornton sneered. "A man's honor is not weighed only in public eyes."

Sudbury pressed his finger against his lips and nodded. "Very true, very true. Well, we are at an impasse, then."

The door flung open and the person entering shrieked in a high voice, "You are giving up already?"

Henry stood. "Charlotte?"

Her attention focused on him like the heated smack of a tutor's stick. "I am not familiar with the rules of a duel, but I cannot imagine giving up on the negotiations so easily when the consequence is physical harm."

Sudbury stood up for himself. "Here now, I say I tried."

Wallace quietly stepped in front of Charlotte, whispering how this had nothing to do with her.

She smacked his arm and stepped around him. "Don't be stupid."

Thornton growled, "Someone get the wench under control."

Henry curled his fingers into a fist but relaxed when he glanced at Charlotte. She hissed, "How dare you enter another man's home and then offend the women in it. No wonder the negotiations aren't working. You don't have any honor to defend."

Henry nodded. "That's the issue."

Thornton had reeled back his arm, but since he must not be completely stupid, he merely brought it up to rub his cheek. "Leave it to a woman to make matters worse."

Charlotte shouldn't be here and Henry knew it. Wallace knew it. She probably knew it, too.

She rounded on Wallace. "This is your fault."

Henry had a mind to step in. Maybe it was the frayed ends of his thoughts that held him back. That and the ferocious sparkle Charlotte radiated, daring one of the men to tell her to do something against her will.

Wallace hung his head and shifted his eyes away, muttering, "I know."

She threw her arms up in the air and turned again, eyeing the rest of the men like a predator eyeing which animal it should make its next meal. "I forbid this."

In the silence of the room, the fire crackled and the soft thud of a piece of wood falling resonated in the fireplace, slightly muffled by the puff of powdery ashes. Henry blinked and something in him reacted with more determination than he had felt in the last ten minutes combined. "Charlotte, I am glad you are here."

He was glad. She shifted his perspective by giving a voice to all the things he cared about.

She said, "So the duel is off. It is settled."

Under his mustache, Thornton's lips stretched in what was probably an oily smile. "This is a matter for the men. Nothing is settled. Mr. Simmons, it is your honor at stake."

Henry said, "Very well. Then I will meet Mr. Burke at dawn, walk my paces, and shoot him. I do not miss."

Charlotte exclaimed, "No!"

Sudbury stroked his chin. "Aye, Henry. If you shoot him, you will probably have to leave the country."

He couldn't leave his land and he certainly didn't want to leave Charlotte. At the time the duel was offered, he had thought about nothing beyond putting the offending vermin in his place. That shining entity inside every gentleman, his sense of pride, told him to uphold his honor, even against someone as disgusting as Mr. Burke. Henry was the better man and upholding his word, proving his skill, and following through with the duel was certainly what any other gentleman would do.

He asked, "Does Mr. Burke plan to delope?"

"No."

"Is there a way to convince him of the usefulness of doing so?"

Thornton sneered, "We are not friends, Mr. Simmons. You underestimate your offense and if you want to live to see the noon sun tomorrow, you will meet Mr. Burke's demands."

Charlotte gasped. "But a second is supposed to negotiate. To try to keep the duel from happening. There must be some way to avoid this."

Thornton didn't even turn his head to acknowledge that Charlotte had spoken. "Mr. Burke is currently locating a surgeon."

Charlotte crossed the short distance between them and pressed her fingers against Henry's arm. He wrapped his other hand over hers, instinctively drawing on the strength of her presence. "There was never any room for negotiation, then."

Charlotte trembled, her brows gathered and her jagged movements reminded him of a scared mare. She burst with another thought almost like a horse that might try to bolt away. "Will none of you discuss this with Katherine? Surely she should have a say in the matter."

Sudbury snorted. Henry felt Charlotte's fingers squeeze and he narrowed his focus on her. "You are right."

Her eyes widened and her mouth dropped open, a surprised breath catching in her throat. He went on, "It is traditional that a woman be kept unaware of a duel. And, traditionally, I am honor-bound to respond to the duel." He smiled down at her and whispered. "You make me want to break the rules, too."

Thornton asked, "You would not defend your honor? Mr. Burke would not let that go."

And that was the real issue. Men like Mr. Burke only responded to shows of strength. If Henry refused the duel, he gave up his chance at putting a man like that in his place.

He sighed and squeezed Charlotte's hand even harder. "At dawn then."

Charlotte turned her pleading gray eyes his way and whispered, "Henry, please."

Her concern washed down him like a warm embrace and he smiled at her. He wished they were alone so he could pull her closer and run his fingers down her back, whispering to her how she could trust him.

He knew exactly where he would send his bullet.

Chapter 19

Charlotte slammed her hand on the table. "You tell me I am right and then you turn around and do the thing you just admitted was wrong!"

He held up a finger. "Wait, I didn't admit it was wrong. I only said that you were right. And now you are letting that go to your head."

She straightened her arms at her sides, her hands curling in anger. "I fail to see the difference."

"Simply because I think you are right does not automatically make my decision wrong."

"At this point, you are wrong until you can prove otherwise."

He held his brandy in front of him. After Thornton left, someone had handed him a brandy. Probably Sudbury.

He hadn't yet taken a sip.

He set down the glass and said, "You are asking me to make quite a few allowances for your behavior."

She shrieked a sound of frustration behind her teeth, sounding a little like a petulant child. He held up a hand, trying to work in a word before she did or said something in a state of temper. "I can explain why my decision is the only way."

She settled a little, her shoulders rolling and dropping, some of the tenacity quieting. "Explain?"

He nodded and stepped forward, treading carefully, worried he would spook her. "A man like Burke does not stop until someone makes him stop. He requires a force greater than himself or he will continue down his path. And right now, Katherine is his target."

She huffed and he could feel the exasperation rolling from her as she tried to contain her fury. "This is Wallace's fight!"

Wallace dropped his arm from the wall and straightened, taking another swig of brandy. "Don't I know that."

Charlotte said, "Then Wallace should, er, Wallace..."

Henry prowled a step closer. "Should Wallace take my place?"

Her eyes flew up to his, widening. He didn't often draw himself up to his full height or use his breadth to intimidate another person. He could see the moment when her eyes dilated and she realized how easy it was for him to invade her personal space.

Then she blinked and her eyes flickered with a small fire. She was still angry and, no matter how intimidating he acted, she wasn't cowed. "My point is that a duel should not happen at all. You don't have to do it."

He tucked a loose curl behind her ear. "If you worry about me, then I will count that as enough worrying for the both of us."

"Oh!" She swatted at his chest. "Now I understand why women stay out of this madness. There is absolutely no getting through to you."

He tapped her chin. "I don't know why we leave women out of these matters. I could be sitting here contemplating the next few hours of my life but instead I get to argue with you."

She smacked his chest again and he caught her wrist, holding it captive against him. She scoffed and then settled and whispered, "He could shoot you."

"You are right again. I should have chosen swords and let him try to stab me."

"That is the point!"

"Of his sword, yes, that is how he would stab me."

Sudbury laughed from his seat. "Careful, Henry, or I will stab you myself. She is right to be worried."

Suddenly her hand darted between the folds of her skirt and she pulled something from a pocket he hadn't even known was there. She held out a coin.

He stared at it while she waved it around and then pushed it at him. "What is this?"

She picked up his hand and placed the coin in his palm. "My lucky coin from dinner."

His fingers closed around it and he hauled her to him, not caring who else was around to see them. There were times when a man had to hang the rules.

Charlotte relaxed and leaned forward, her hand resting heavier on his chest. Her lips were so close now and, she was right, he could be shot at in a few hours. Like lightning, something sizzled down his body and he had the sudden urge to capture her. To make the most of the next few hours.

Sudbury interrupted, "Are you going to kiss or not?"

At the same time, Wallace barked, "Simmons!"

Charlotte smiled and raised herself up to meet his lips.

THE FROZEN EARTH SLEPT under a blanket of snow that glowed violet under the first rays of light. The sky was splashed a dozen different hues from indigo to ochre and under it all, the men were arranged on the shoveled gravel drive, shadowy forms with distinct characteristics. Sudbury wore his hat tilted at an angle and Henry's cape whipped around in the wind.

From the window, she could see Sudbury hand a pistol to Henry and her heart thumped in her throat, constricting the airflow to her lungs. Panic set in on her like a frenzied beast and she ran to the door.

They told her to stay in the house, away from the bullets, but how could she sit here, safe, when he was not? Until this moment, the duel had been an idea, a future activity that caused worry. But the sight of Henry holding a pistol sent shivers of fear down her spine.

Katherine called after her. "Charlotte! Charlotte, you will miss it!"

"I have to stop it!"

The butler blocked the door, shaking his head at her. "Miss."

She trembled in the hall, hesitating and hating herself for it. She could push him aside and dart out.

Could she?

Katherine called again. "Come back to the window. Or, better, yet, come sit with me."

Charlotte shook her head, a pin that had held all night came loose and another lock of hair tumbled down the side of her face. As if the pin had been the only tiny thing holding back her emotions, she suddenly sobbed and ran back to the window, trying to squint through her tears.

Out on the drive, Henry and Burke walked away from each other. Suddenly, the men turned and there was a loud crack, like an old tree falling, but magnified in a way that shook her soul. Charlotte cried out, the sound of the shot gripping her in stasis as she watched Henry and waited to see if he fell.

He hadn't lifted his arm, yet, and her focus swiveled over to Burke. He stood with a smoking pistol, his arm extended, and a sly grin on his face. Charlotte couldn't breathe and she realized they were all waiting for the same thing.

For Henry to fall.

His cape, whipping in the wind, pulled aside to show his arms still by his sides, his finger ready on his pistol. Slowly, agonizingly slowly, his face grim, he lifted his arm and pointed the gun at Burke.

Henry hadn't taken his shot, yet.

And he was still standing.

Charlotte whimpered.

Burke's arm lowered and he backed up a step. He held up his hands, palms out in front of him, the pistol dangling from his fingers. She couldn't hear any words from here, but she felt a small thrill in seeing the panic wash over the face of the man who had shot at the man she loved.

Burke's lips moved, pleading. For every cowardly step back, Henry's feet moved forward with practiced grace, his pistol never wavering.

Charlotte twisted her fingers together, the sickening feeling of potential death sliding down her. Everything about this was wrong. If Henry shot Burke now, it would take a kind of cold-heartedness Charlotte didn't possess.

Burke dropped his gun and his face scrunched. It looked like he might be crying, but he stopped backing away, stood straight, and faced Henry with squared shoulders, his eyes squeezed shut.

Another crack resonated through the world, hitting everything it touched with a sense of shock, almost holding time still until the sound faded.

Charlotte could count her heartbeats, they were nearly bursting from her chest.

Burke still stood and Henry held his pistol out and up.

He hadn't shot Burke.

He had deloped.

Burke sank to his knees, unsettling some light snowflakes that drifted around him, swirling in the wind.

Charlotte had never been so close to fainting.

It was over.

Chapter 20

It was understandable that the elder Mrs. Burke left that morning in a storm of sniping and scowls. Aunt Johanna saw her friend off and after, Charlotte caught her aunt doing something she had never seen before.

Slumping against the wall.

Gingerly, she touched her aunt's shoulder. She wasn't sure what to say, so she kept silent until Aunt Johanna opened her eyes and stood up straight. Then, as if the moment had never happened, she walked down the hall, her shoes clacking over the marble.

Mr. Lawton and his daughter were the next ones to leave. Emma hugged Charlotte and promised to write, declaring she would never want to lose a friend who had so much drama to share.

Charlotte wanted to melt onto the floor, denying that drama had anything to do with her.

Emma merely grinned, checked her hat, stuffed her hands into her fur muff, and then left with a few words of good wishes.

Sudbury strode into the hall, pulling on his hat and looking rather debonair for a man who had been up all night. Charlotte supposed it was something he was used to.

He said, "Well, my dear, I am off as well."

"Why are you not leaving with Henry?"

"I have decided to travel home for a brief reprieve. I must head to London soon and think I will, as they say, convalesce."

She laughed, doubting him. "You? Convalesce?"

He grinned, a naughty grin that probably made the ladies of London swoon. "I am capable of being a good boy for a short time."

Charlotte doubted that, too.

He gathered her hands and pressed them between his own. "I wish you luck, Miss Moore."

She blushed and averted her eyes from his pressing gaze. "Thank you, Lord Sudbury."

He backed away and nodded once at her before leaving.

Four down, only two left.

Katherine would stay for now, so Charlotte amended her count.

Only one left.

He entered the hall, looking down at his gloves, flipping them back and forth between his bare hands. He was too broad to look boyish, but he did look thoughtful and a little subdued.

"Henry?"

He looked up at her and his smile of relief tugged at her heart. She would not have missed his departure.

He said, "I think it best I leave. My godmother is not happy with me and it is probably safest to depart sooner than planned."

A part of Charlotte wanted to laugh at his understatement. Aunt Johanna was livid. But a stronger part of her understood what it meant to Henry. He had done the opposite of everything his godmother had expected of him. He was not engaged

to an heiress and he had caused a scandal at her party by partic-
ipating in a duel. On Christmas, no less.

At least he still stood here today.

She stepped forward and he met her halfway, wrapping his
arms around her shoulders and nuzzling into her hair. His heat
felt warm and welcome in the chilly hall and she rested her
forehead against him, softening into the comfort of his embrace.

She needed this. She needed someone who knew her, who
knew who she really was and wanted her anyway.

She wasn't a perfect lady and probably never would be.

His voice raspy with emotion and muffled by her hair, he
said, "I don't want to let you go. I want to carry you away in my
arms."

She wrapped her arms around him a little tighter. "I feel
the same way. When you leave, I have to go back to a world in
which I am not accepted by the people around me."

A voice rang clear from the stairs. "That is not true, my
dear."

She stepped back. "Aunt Johanna?"

Her aunt slid a gloved hand down the banister, her black
lace skirt trailing behind her. "Have you been so unhappy with
me these few years?"

Charlotte hesitated. That was the very thing she had re-
cently been pondering. She was finally relieved to give an honest answer. "I have been content here with you."

Her aunt nodded. "Yes. I suppose. I know both of you very
well." Her eyes raked over Charlotte and Henry. "As far as fi-
nances are concerned, you two do not suit. But as far as all the
other things that will make you happy, you two are perfect to-

gether. I cannot deny that and so that is what I will tell your mother."

Inside, it felt as if a small piece Charlotte had not known was loose was pushed back into place. "Aunt Johanna, you support our decision?"

"I do. And, since scandal follows you anyway, my dear, at the extreme end of things, I would support a long trip to make sure you get what you want."

Henry asked, "Are you suggesting Gretna Green?"

She winked. "Oh, I would never say anything that scandalous."

She turned and left the hall for her study.

Henry tangled his fingers between Charlotte's and lifted her hand to his lips. "I didn't know, until last night, how good it could feel to have someone on my side. Someone with me, caring about me. I thought before that we would work well together, but now I think, perhaps, having faced a bullet, my feelings are stronger than I knew. I think I love you."

She was trying to suck in a breath, but it was difficult to think of much else while his lips left a warm trail over her skin. "And you don't mind that I broke the rules?"

Did he just lick her thumb? She might melt, right here in the hall.

He said, "I think we can make and follow our own rules. Together. I will take you skating and sledding and horseback riding and dancing and over dinner, we will plan our lives to be the way we want them to be."

No more pretending to be docile? No more feigning interest in dull activities? She could exercise and plan and share her ideas? Henry would listen to her, accept her, and love her for it all the more.

"You really think you love me?"

He tugged her closer and she giggled. Maybe they were a little scandalous. He said, "I do. I really think I love you."

She rested the back of her fingers against the side of his face, her heart fluttering in her chest. "I love you, too."

The butler cleared his throat and held out Henry's cape. "Your horse is ready, sir."

Before donning his cape, Henry pulled the silver coin out of an inner pocket and handed it to her, folding her fingers over it and covering her hand between his. "I kept this close to my heart the entire time. For one terrible moment, I was sure the bullet was coming straight for me. Maybe a Christmas coin is luckier than we will ever know."

He pecked a last kiss on her cheek before stepping away.

Throwing the cape over his shoulders, he smiled at her. The fabric fanned out behind him and Charlotte noticed the light filter through a small, round hole in the black fabric.

Epilogue

Everything felt different now that she was home. She had missed her siblings, missed the comfort of her old wool blanket, missed dinners with her family.

She also missed extracting Henry's smile, the soft touches he would sneak in the drawing room, and the comfort she felt wrapped in his love and acceptance.

She didn't know who to be now that she was home. She was still Charlotte, but not quite. She felt as if someone had dampened her spirits like smothering a fire. It didn't feel the same to share jokes with her sister or play pranks on their brother and they both pouted at her, insisting she was no fun anymore.

Maybe she wasn't.

But with her aunt, her focus had shifted. Now she saw tackling a responsibility and finishing a chore with a sense of pride and her thoughts often drifted to all of her conversations with Henry and the things he wanted to do to his home.

Out in the garden, the April sunshine warmed her cheeks even as the winter chill hung in the air. Her mother spoke with a servant, leaving Charlotte to wander alone in the barely budding rose bushes.

Someone from the house called her name and she squinted over. Squealing and lifting her skirts, she ran. "Henry!"

Behind her, she heard her mother's admonishment but it quickly rinsed off as Charlotte was determined nothing could ruin her exaltation. Colliding into his large chest, it felt like home to be wrapped in his arms.

He kissed the top of her head. "I spoke with your father."

She tilted her head to look up at him. "And?"

"And, if it is amenable, then I will stay while the banns are read, or if you would prefer we can exchange letters for a while or-"

She squealed again. "Henry!"

He grinned. "Charlotte, will you marry me?"

"Yes! Yes! Yes!"

He squeezed her to him and spun around, her feet swinging out and laughter bubbling freely.

Henry set her down and kissed her cheek. "I cannot wait to spend my life with you."

She slipped her hand in his, unwilling to let go of him yet. "We are going to have so much fun together."

<hr>

NEXT IN SERIES: *Miss Locke's Christmas Secret*

Thank you for reading and I hope you enjoyed the novella. If so, please leave me a review so others know you enjoyed my work. A recommendation from another reader (you!) means so much! Thank you! If you would like to read more of my work, please visit me at www.anastasiahistoricals.com[1] where you can also sign up for my newsletter :)

Excerpt from Miss Locke's Christmas Secret

That's it, Amelia. Think of all the exhausting things your mother will drag you to tomorrow and you will...

She blew out the candle.

...be able to close your eyes...

She snuggled her head into her downy pillow.

...and rest your mind...

She tried to stop worrying about everything all at once.

...and theoretically, you will fall asleep.

She heard the soft sound of her door opening. Then there was a tiny metallic sound of the latch falling back into place to close the door.

A husky, male voice floated across her bedroom, "Well, do I have a surprise for you."

Eyes wide, staring at the dark wall, wishing she was facing the door, she wondered what to do. Should she scream? Should she roll out of bed and run for the fire poker?

His voice sounded closer, now. "Are you asleep? I have ways to wake you up."

She knew this voice. He sounded so familiar. Who was it?

"Tsk, tsk, Mary. How could you invite me and then fall asleep?"

Mary? He was meeting her mother?

No, that didn't make any sense.

She rolled from bed, sliding from under the covers, and darted to the fireplace to grab the poker. "Get out of my room!"

She yelled it. The walls of this house were horridly thin and sounds carried easily. Someone would rescue her at any moment.

He screamed. "Gah! You're not Mary!"

At the same time, she blinked and blurted out a startled realization. "Lord Sudbury?"

This man was a cad! He must have misunderstood her mother's natural inclination to flirt and taken it as an invitation.

What a bounder! A completely dishonest, selfish, immoral...

She raised her poker higher. "Get out!"

Read more about Miss Locke and Lord Sudbury at the next Christmas party in *Miss Locke's Christmas Secret.*

Printed in Great Britain
by Amazon